I Kissed a Frog

Rupa Gulab is a columnist and author. She firmly believes that it's much, much more fun to laugh than cry and get puffy eyes and a bright red nose like Rudolph the reindeer. Fortunately, in retrospect, almost anything is funny, right?

Also by Rupa Gulab

Girl Alone (2005)

Chip of the Old Blockhead (2006)

The Great Depression of the 40s: A Novel (2010)

I Kissed a Frog

Rupa Gulab

PAN BOOKS

First published in the Indian subcontinent 2013 by Pan
an imprint of Pan Macmillan,
a division of Macmillan Publishers Limited
Pan Macmillan, 20 New Wharf Road, London N1 9RR
Basingstoke and Oxford
Associated companies throughout the world
www.panmacmillan.com

ISBN 978-93-82616-05-4

1 3 5 7 9 8 6 4 2

Typeset in 10.5/13.8 ITC Giovanni by InoSoft Systems, Noida
Printed and bound in India by Thomson Press India Ltd.

For people who hate lizards and
cockroaches as much as I do.
Oh and, um, frogs too.

Contents

Love and Other Four-letter Words

1

Hell's Angel

My relationship with Varun ended abruptly at my best friend Tanya's wedding. Okay, I was the one who played Terminator, but I was feeling desperately ill and in no mood to deal with the intense, life-changing conversation Varun had brought up. I still hadn't recovered from the night out with the girls – and that was forty-eight hours ago. Chasing vodka with tequila shots seemed like an excellent idea then, but I'm older and wiser now. Never again.

Tanya was looking as ill as I was feeling, which was odd because she'd just had a small vodka on that girlie night – she'd said she didn't want puffy eyes on her big day. She still had puffy eyes, though. They were red-rimmed, too, and brimming with tears. She wept uncontrollably when I went to the hotel to help her get dressed.

'Oh help Diya, I can't go through with this!'

'Have you, like, lost it?' I demanded. 'This is the

guy you wanted to marry since you were fifteen years old! You even told me idiotic things like the names of the babies you were going to have with him. Get a grip, woman!'

'That was then, this is now,' she wailed.

I sighed. My head was throbbing so hard, I just couldn't deal with theatrics. The only person I could sympathize with right then was myself.

'And why have you gone off him? Has someone suddenly slapped him with a paternity suit or what?' I said waspishly. 'It's just nerves, Tanya. I've read somewhere that it's normal to get them on your wedding day. *Everyone* does! For all you know, Sanjay's probably having second thoughts too. Hey, he could well be on his way to the airport now to buy himself a one-way ticket to Ibiza or someplace else where chicks are hot and easy.'

This made her cry even louder.

'You're the one who told me I was a fool to marry the only man I've ever dated,' Tanya wailed accusingly.

Guilty as charged. But I'd just been teasing her – I really, really liked Sanjay. And now she was threatening to dump him on her wedding day because of stupid old me. How *could* I do this to my best friend – the person who had comforted me and kept me sane in boarding school after my parents got divorced? I owed her big time.

After mentally kicking myself, I took a bold step to retrieve the situation. Admittedly, it was a bit of a gamble.

'Okay,' I shrugged. 'Dump him, then, if that's what you really want. And hey, let's drink to that!'

Tanya looked dumbstruck as I took a mini bottle of vodka out of the fridge, poured the contents into two glasses and lustily said, 'Cheers!'

She echoed me in a weak and wavering voice, but I pretended not to notice.

'So, are you going to tell him or do you want me to do it? After all, that's what friends are for, right?' I said cheerfully.

She was silent. Perfect. This was my cue to make my killer move.

'The best thing is, you won't feel guilty forever. I mean, Sanjay's not bad-looking so I'm sure he'll be snapped up soon. And then there's that woman at his office, the one you absolutely hate, who looks at him with naked lust in her eyes. She'll be over the moon!'

A strangled sob is all I got in response. I turned my face away from Tanya to hide my triumphant grin. After composing my face into a deeply concerned Hollywood-star-talking-to-rolling-cameras-about-orphans-in-Africa expression, I faced Tanya and enveloped her in a bear hug.

'Do you love him?' I asked gently.

'Of *course*, Diya!' she muttered petulantly.

'Aha, thought so! I love him too, so cheers to that!' I crowed.

Her face brightened instantly and she took a gulp of the vodka. I followed suit and grimaced. My stomach churned and I knew in a flash that hair of the dog does not work – do *not* try it! Fortunately, I also darted to the loo in a flash, or else Tanya's gorgeous wedding sari would have been drenched with puke.

The wedding ceremony was beautiful. Tanya didn't shed a single tear, and instead of sedately walking around the fire in a demure manner, she was sprinting with excitement. Varun was so inspired he squeezed my hand and asked me to marry him. I said no. Firmly. Hello, I'm only twenty-seven! I need to live a little before I settle down. Also, I want to be absolutely sure about the man I marry; after witnessing the acrimonious divorce battles my parents went through, I'm very clear that when I settle down with someone it's going to be for the rest of my life.

Later that night I sobbed into my pillow. Not over Varun – god, he's just one of those random men who come and go, but for my best and only friend

Tanya. She was going to live miles away in New York from tomorrow. I was dead certain I wouldn't survive without her. I mean, she's the only person on planet Earth who gets me!

When I got to office late on Monday morning, the restroom was buzzing with excitement: there was a new guy at work! This was marvellous news, considering that about 95 per cent of the people at my office are women – it's almost like being in a convent. This is one of the pitfalls of working for a glamour magazine. Trust me, it's not as cool as it sounds.

The girls were elbowing each other out of the way to get to the mirror. Make-up was touched up, buttons were sexily unbuttoned and even mousy Gitanjali, who never wore anything more daring than tinted lip gloss, was applying fire-engine red lipstick!

'Seriously, he's that hot?' I asked, astonished.

There was an orgasmic chorus of 'Yes! Yes! Oooh yes!'

Wonderful, I thought glumly. The day I decide to wear baggy jeans and a grungy tee an ex had left in my apartment (I don't remember which ex, exactly), a hottie pops up.

'Gimme that tarty lipstick when you're done with it, Gitanjali,' I pleaded.

'No way, Diya,' she glared. 'You're infuriatingly sexy already, give the rest of us a chance!'

As usual, everyone enthusiastically agreed with her, including my frenemy Anushka, who had unbuttoned her shirt almost to her navel.

I gave up. It's not easy having fabulously long legs and high cheekbones – I mean, guys absolutely worship you for it but girls just can't stand you, they're kinder to serial killers and that's a fact. The worst part is, the jealous girls secretly console themselves that every attractive woman must be a brain-dead bimbo. So not fair!

I reached my desk just in time. I'd barely sat down when the HR head came up to my cubicle – she was introducing the new guy to everyone at work. I took one look at him, and omigod, I immediately wanted to rush back to my apartment and change into something else – like my little black dress with the plunging neckline. Thank god I'd dumped Varun the night before!

My next instinct was to call Tanya and tell her all about the new hottie's spiky brown hair, amazing bod and irresistible pheromones. I whipped out my cell phone and midway through dialling her number remembered that she was on a flight to

New York. Rats! If I didn't like Sanjay so much, I could have killed him for taking my best friend far, far away.

A spot of invaluable advice for employers – if you want your employees to really enjoy their jobs, add glamour to the office by hiring a few smoking hot men and women. Rehan, the new guy at work, gave most of us a reason (the best reason ever) to come to office daily! Oh, he was so good at it – he flirted shamelessly with all of us.

There was serious betting going on at the office: who would Rehan ask out first? I was hugely flattered when Mavis, the Senior Editor's secretary, whispered to me that her boss, my boss and several VPs had put big money on me. Everybody knows that secretaries are the most reliable source of office information: they can tell you whose cabin was used for a one-night stand, and colourful details like whether the condoms were ribbed, dotted or strawberry-flavoured. Mavis's encouraging words inspired me to try a little harder with Rehan – I mean, I couldn't let all those important senior people down. I started wearing skirts the size of my dad's handkerchiefs and slinky little tops to office. It certainly got me a lot of unwelcome attention on my way to work and back, but that annoying Rehan still didn't pay more attention to me than he did to the other girls.

Anushka was trying as hard as I was. She even tried to shame me into giving up the battle for Rehan.

'You're dating Varun already, Diya, so back off.'

I snorted. 'Varun is ancient history now, so you back off!'

After all that excitement, you'll never guess who Rehan asked out first: a hairy thing with a Rajput moustache who worked in the accounts department. Omigod, Rehan was gloriously gay – no wonder he asked me where I got my fishnet stockings from!

Naturally, the next day all the women wore gloomy looks and sensible clothes. It was pointless coming to work semi-undressed since we'd discovered Rehan's secret – it truly is tragic that most of the best-looking men in the world are gay.

I was furious because all the top-management types who had bet solid money that Rehan would ask *me* out first were sore losers – they glowered and glared at me all day! To make matters worse, a client whose company manufactured sanitary napkins asked me out on a sort of date.

'Good news, Diya, we need to do an advertorial on my product for the next issue. I'm thinking six pages. Let's go for a drink tonight and discuss it,' Rahul Singh said at the meeting.

'Um, ah, can't we discuss it now?' I mumbled, trying hard to invent a plausible excuse to wriggle out. See, I like Rahul. He's cute and amusing, but he's about forty kg overweight. I refuse to be seen with him in public in case people think we're a couple – so I'm shallow, big deal! Besides, I hate advertorials. They don't bring in as much money as ads do, and you have to practically go down on your knees and beg the editorial department to work on them instead of churning out ditzy articles like 'How to Turn Your Boyfriend into Your Sex Slave'. Honestly, I hate the editorial department. They act like divas because they're the talent and treat ad sales people with contempt, as though we're the lowest critters in the food chain. I always feel indignant when they put us down – I mean, if it weren't for the ads we bring in, the mag would fold up.

'That's an excellent idea, Rahul,' my boss cut in crisply before Rahul could respond. 'And, anyway, Diya's got nothing special lined up for the evening,' she said waspishly. Stupid old bat! She was just getting back at me because she'd lost a lot of money in the Rehan gamble. I *know* she did – Mavis told me!

I attacked Rehan when he popped up at my desk later and attempted to flirt with me.

'Darling, how come you're dressed like a nun today?' he said.

'Because I'm getting none from you,' I muttered irritably.

'And what does that mean?' Rehan looked puzzled.

'It means you're gay so stop wasting my time!' I snapped.

He looked startled first and annoyed later.

'Excuse me, I'm so not gay!'

'Really? So why did you go out with that accounts guy last night?'

'WTF? I went out with him because there's a screw-up in my cost-to-company letter and I need it sorted out ASAP. Hell, money's more important than women!'

And then he asked me out for a drink and I remembered that I already had a date with the sanitary-napkin client that night. Damn.

Oh well, after my initial panic died down I figured things out. I wasn't particularly perturbed that I had two dates to juggle – I've handled mess-ups like that before. What bothered me more was that I didn't have time to change into something nice that evening – I had to be wined and dined in the Hell's Angels tee I'd groggily slipped on for office that morning. To compensate for my grungy attire, I laid on the make-up real thick with Cleopatra-style eyeliner and other interesting touches, so at the end of it all I looked casual but chic. Sort of like those models in Diesel ads.

When Rahul and I settled down at a corner table he'd chosen, I told him that I had to leave at 9.30 pm.

'Or else Cinderella will turn into an orange pumpkin?' he teased.

'Nah, orange just isn't me. Seriously, though, I have to work on a business pitch for a perfume client tonight,' I lied.

Rahul bought my excuse without raising an eyebrow.

'Right, then, let's get the advertorial discussion over with before time runs out. The most important thing about our brand of sanitary napkins is the super-soak technology,' he began.

I groaned inwardly. Here I was sipping a divine Bloody Mary in a posh restaurant with a sea view, and my companion wanted to discuss soggy, squelchy sanitary napkins.

I mentally tuned out, pretending to listen.

When I couldn't take it any more, I told Rahul that instead of focusing so heavily on the super-soak technology and boring things like weaves, suppose our advertorial was a little more reader-friendly?

'I mean, we can carry interesting articles on pre-menstrual stress and suchlike,' I suggested.' I kept my fingers crossed as I said that. The editorial department wouldn't kick up too much of a fuss over articles like that. Pre-menstrual stress is a subject women enjoy moaning and groaning about. Seriously.

'Nope, that's too generic,' Rahul said firmly. 'Our technology has absolutely got to be the star – it's what makes us the No. 1 brand worldwide.'

I stared at him glumly. Rahul noted my expression with an audible sigh. He shook his head exasperatedly.

'Okay, let's see if I can make you as enthused about it as I am,' he said decisively, and my eyes widened with horror as he whipped a sanitary napkin out of his jacket pocket. Heck, what sort of man keeps sanitary napkins in his pocket?

He placed it on his crumb-speckled quarter plate, picked up my Bloody Mary and poured it over the sanitary napkin. My jaw dropped to my ankles.

'Have you lost it? You can't do this in a public place!' I hissed urgently.

He ignored my protests and concentrated deeply on the sanitary napkin.

'Look at it soaking up that Bloody Mary! Isn't it bloody marvellous?' he said excitedly.

I have to admit that it did such a good job, I made a mental note to switch to Dry Days (that's what Rahul's brand was called).

Rahul disgusted me further by prodding the sanitary napkin with a finger.

'See how dry it is within seconds? Go on, touch it!' he urged.

I touched it gingerly – I had no choice. I agreed that it was dry and made a feeble joke about it being ironic that a product called Dry Days had soaked up an alcoholic beverage.

Rahul wasn't listening to me. He was still staring raptly at the sanitary napkin. I saw a waiter approaching and hurriedly snatched the sanitary napkin off Rahul's plate and bundled it into my table napkin.

I thought better of handing over the embarrassing package to Rahul – he was capable of exposing the sanitary napkin again – so I shoved it into the outside pocket of my handbag.

Rahul leaned back in his chair with an air of deep satisfaction.

'So now do you understand why the advertorial has to focus on the super-soak technology instead of frippery things like PMS?' Rahul asked.

I still didn't agree with him but I nodded. I silently resolved to debate this with him further in a more private place, like his office cabin.

'Great! Oh, and sorry about pinching your Bloody Mary,' Rahul said without looking remotely apologetic.

'Yes, that was mean of you,' I said severely. 'You could have poured your own drink on it.'

'What, waste my precious single malt?' Rahul looked horrified. 'Besides, your drink was more appropriate, keeping the name and colour in mind. The consistency, too, if you consider heavy clotting days,' he said and started looking dreamy-eyed again.

I didn't want to know where this would lead, so I cut him short.

'I'm starving. Can we order the mains now?' I slimily knew that this would distract Rahul. Food is his greatest love.

He summoned the waiter and ordered three Hyderabadi biryanis. As I raised my eyebrows he said, 'One for you and two for me.' There wasn't a trace of embarrassment on his face.

'You seriously should go on a diet,' I told him sternly.

'Impossible! That's like asking a smoker to quit,' he shrugged.

Right then, I got a text message from Rehan: 'At Turquoise Toad with Anushka. Take your time.'

I lost it completely. I told Rahul that I had to use the restroom urgently and dashed out to the street, hailing a cab. There was no way I was going to let Anushka steal the hottest guy at office from me!

I sent an apologetic text message to Rahul, of course: 'Sudden asthma attack, gone home. So sorry.'

Admittedly, I did feel guilty about ditching Rahul at the restaurant, but I consoled myself with the thought that instead of just two biryanis, he could eat three – I'm sure that made him terrifically happy.

All I was focused on was getting to Turquoise Toad fast, before predatory Anushka could sink her claws into Rehan – *my* Rehan! Damn the Mumbai traffic – it took me almost thirty-five minutes to get there. My heart sank when I walked in and saw Rehan and Anushka leaning intimately towards each other across a table. And then it soared sky-high when Rehan looked up and noticed me: I can swear his eyes lit up like firecrackers. Anushka gave me a tight smile that barely hid her annoyance. I smiled sweetly in return and said, 'Hey, thanks for entertaining Rehan while I was with the client.' What I was implying was, 'Thanks for warming my seat – now get up and leave!' She didn't take the hint, rats!

With Anushka around, it was a completely pointless date. While part of me gave Rehan full marks for being gentlemanly and paying equal attention to both of us, the other part of me wanted to shake him till his teeth rattled. All my hopes for a cozy getting-to-know-each-other twosome went up in smoke.

Soon after, I felt a real asthma attack coming on when I noticed Rahul with a bunch of people at the table bang opposite me. 'Let's go, I'm feeling ill,' I wheezed frantically. At that very moment, Rahul's eyes met mine. He looked fleetingly hurt. Then he turned his head away and shoved a family-sized burger into his mouth. Two things struck me simultaneously: how on earth did he find the space to eat any more after three heavy biryanis? And god, if he mentions this to my marketing head, I'm probably going to lose my job!

I tossed and turned all night. Not just because Rehan had enthusiastically agreed to come home for dinner the next day. Every time I tried to plan the menu in my head (wine, oysters, strawberries, dark chocolate, et cetera), Rahul's face would pop in uninvited – and that hurt expression on it would kill me. Right, so I'm not a very nice person, but I'm not evil either. Also, I was terrified about losing my job – some clients can be spiteful, particularly when you dump them in the middle of dinner.

At 4 am I decided to call Rahul and apologize, and composed several messages in my head. I finally made the call at 8.30 am. I stuttered the whole truth and, after he heard me out, he laughed uproariously. 'Jesus, you really lived up to that Hell's Angels tee you wore last night – my god, you're a bloody handful,' he guffawed.

'I said I'm sorry,' I repeated in a constrained voice.

'No sweat, Diya, though you should have told me – I'd have been cool with it! Come on, why would you want to spend the evening with fat, ugly old me when you had a date with a stud?'

'Hey, you're not ugly!' I protested. 'Lose at least forty kg and you'll look like a stud too.' That part really was true. Rahul had the face of a Greek god with dimples and all, and the body of an elephant.

'Oooh, don't stop – I so love flattery,' Rahul said with a laugh.

When I hung up my conscience was clear and I was focused on Rehan and Rehan alone. After a quick trip to the shops, I did the house and myself up. I'm happy to say that my apartment looked cozily warm and I looked sizzling hot! When the doorbell finally rang and I opened the door, my welcoming smile froze. There was a very tall, large girl with suitcases and a violin standing outside.

She smiled politely as I raised my eyebrows. 'Hey there, I'm Mallika, your new flatmate,' she said apologetically. Oh god, the landlady had warned me but I'd forgotten! Rats, could I never have a private date with Rehan? I fleetingly wondered whether while showing Mallika her room, I could swiftly shove her in and lock the door!

I did the next best thing – I begged her to stay in her room voluntarily instead. Mallika was very understanding when I bitterly informed her that she had ruined my date.

'Oops, sorry – promise I won't intrude,' she apologized.

Rehan and I had a super-romantic time – and just when we were on our fourth glass of wine, the doorbell rang. At midnight!

It was a pizza delivery man with the largest pizza ever. Heck, I hadn't ordered pizza!

'For Mallika Nair,' he informed me. I paid grumpily and, as I was knocking at her door, Rehan sighed.

'Mmm, smells like pepperoni. I'd kill for a slice of that!'

Mallika opened the door just then and generously said, 'You can have two slices, if you want. As long as you give me some of that dark chocolate mousse Diya has made in exchange.'

'Deal!' Rehan said, without consulting me. The cheek!

'Pop in then,' Mallika ushered us into her room. 'I promised Diya that I'd stay here till you left and I always keep my word.' She looked like she had a halo shimmering over her head as she said that.

So all three of us sat on her single bed and I didn't mind it any more when I realized that I was squashed against Rehan. I mean, Mallika took up most of the bed, hooray! He put an arm around me and I was in heaven.

'Gosh, you play the violin? Hey, why don't you serenade us?' Rehan said when he noticed her violin case on a chair.

'Sure,' Mallika agreed, and I snuggled closer to Rehan when she got up. This was going better than I'd planned – till Mallika started playing 'Three Blind Mice'!

'Hello, don't you know anything more romantic?' I squawked.

'Nope,' Mallika shrugged. 'I just started learning a few months ago. I always take up new hobbies when I'm dumped. I've done goldfish, bonsai and now this. The creep left me for a skinny underwear model,' she added, and suddenly burst into tears.

I always fall back on clichés when my female friends are dumped. 'Men are bastards,' I consoled Mallika sympathetically. She wailed louder and corrected me. '*All* men are bastards!' she spat out and stamped her foot.

'Dammit, that's not fair,' Rehan said vehemently. 'I'm a man and I'm not a bastard,' he added feebly as Mallika glared at him.

'Oh really?' she said coldly. 'So tell me, have you never lied to any of your girlfriends about working late when you were actually romancing another babe?'

I looked at Rehan curiously and discovered that he was beetroot red.

'Um,' he said nervously.

'Is that a yes or a no?' Mallika thundered.

'Um, yes,' Rehan said looking shame-faced. 'But in my defence, I only do that when I know the relationship is over in my head.'

I jumped in. I was pretty angry now. The 'all-men-are-bastards' mantra can really get women worked up.

'So why don't you tell your girlfriends that the relationship is over *before* you date other women? You know what? I bet you don't tell them before because you want to check out the new babe to see if she really is better than the current one. Douchebag!'

The only applause I got for my passionate speech was from Mallika. Rehan looked absolutely furious as he made for the door.

'Where are you going?' I asked, alarmed.

'Back to my current girlfriend,' he said coldly. 'She's way better than the new babe I was checking out just now.'

I gasped as I heard the front door slam.

'Omigod, was he serious? Like, does he really have a girlfriend he was cheating on, or did he say that to rile me?' I frantically asked Mallika.

'How does it matter?' Mallika said coolly. 'Remember, all men are bastards.'

I panicked and called Rehan, but his cell phone rang unanswered.

'Ah, forget him, Diya,' Mallika said as she offered me a glass of my own wine. 'Let's drink to ourselves tonight.'

So we did just that and giggled till the newspaper man rang the bell.

While I was dying to call Rehan the next afternoon, I held back. I'll be damned if I'm going to chase men – particularly touchy men who take offence at normal 'all-men-are-bastards' girlie banter. My plan was to make Rehan beg for forgiveness – oh, and dump his girlfriend, too, if he really did have one. There's only one way to do this in my shallow books: a beauty-parlour session and shopping!

An apologetic Mallika accompanied me and even paid for my new haircut. 'I absolutely insist, Diya,' she said. 'After all, I was responsible for your fight.' I found a fabulously sexy outfit and Mallika's expression when I stepped out of the changing room to get her opinion was deeply gratifying. She gasped, 'Omigod, if I were a man I'd die for you!' As I twirled around in a model-like way, a male voice boomed in my ear.

'Me, too! I'd definitely die for Diya.'

It was Rahul's voice; I turned around and simpered.

'But you wouldn't go on a diet for me, would you?' I teased.

'Death is easier than a diet, sweetheart,' was his swift retort.

'Rot! And what are you doing in a female store, you dirty old man?' I wagged a finger at him.

'I promised to take my mum shopping,' he said and pointed towards a former Miss India winner. I recognized her instantly because she used to be a shampoo model in my growing-up years. Gosh, she looked beautiful even at sixty!

'That's your mum?' I gaped. 'No wonder your features are so fabulous!'

Rahul grinned. 'Oh, you think I'm hot, hmm?'

'Not now,' I said patiently, 'but if you lose weight rest assured I'll be ringing your doorbell in a frenzied manner.' I really think I would. I mean, he looked a lot like his mum. That's gosh-darned supermodel material!

'I know we haven't been introduced yet, but I'd like to ring your doorbell right now,' Mallika said saucily.

Rahul laughed and held out his right hand, 'I'm Rahul.'

Mallika smiled coyly as she shook his hand.

My god, she really had a crush on him. For the rest of the evening, Rahul was all she could talk about.

Before she tucked herself into bed that night, she wryly said, 'I think I'm going to be dreaming about Rahul tonight. And I know I'm wasting my time because he's got a thing for you.'

'Rubbish! He just enjoys teasing me, that's all,' I stoutly said.

Mallika stuck to her guns, 'Hello, I can tell these things – believe me, he has a major, major, major crush on you.'

'Hmm, "crush" is the right word to use. My god, he's so overweight that if he so much as hugged me, my bones would turn to liquid!'

'Goodnight, meanie,' Mallika yawned.

I was really looking forward to a long face-to-face chat with Tanya on Skype – I desperately needed my best friend's advice on how to deal with the Rehan situation, but the silly girl wasn't available. I sent her a piteous e-mail, chiding her for forgetting me.

Then, I set my alarm for 5.30 am on Monday morning. It takes hours to look good and I was determined to knock Rehan's socks off. I felt pleased at all the compliments I received from my male colleagues – my new haircut and sexy clothes were working, yay! I was humming a happy song when I bumped into Rehan – the sod didn't even bother to mumble an apology. He glared instead and briskly marched right past me.

My confidence crumbled. Just before lunch break, Anushka came to my desk and brazenly asked if she could borrow my electric orange lipstick for a touch-up. 'Going someplace special?' I asked as I handed it to her. 'Nope. But I'm going with someone special!' she smirked. 'Hey, can you do up my eyes the Cleopatra way you've done yours today? Puhleez?' she pleaded.

'Sure thing,' I shrugged. I mean, why not, I badly needed a distraction. I noticed that the clingy cropped tee she was wearing had ridden up to expose her navel, and there was a stray hair that waved in the gentle air-con breeze like a feisty blade of grass. I made a mental note to whip out my tweezers and pluck it out when I was done with her eyes. I mean, tacky stuff like that can put a date off.

It was only after I finished her make-up that Anushka told me who that someone special was: Rehan! 'I spent all of Sunday with him,' she giggled. 'And we even got to second base.' Holy shit – and to think that I spent all of my Sunday shopping extravagantly to turn that creep on!

I was sunk in gloom; my only bright spot was the fact that I hadn't dealt with Anushka's tacky navel hair after she told me she was dating Rehan – serves her right! And when, during my client meeting with

Rahul he told me that I looked super glam, my eyes involuntarily filled with tears.

'What's the matter?' he asked, alarmed.

'I've been dumped,' I mumbled.

'By that idiot at work, I assume. Look, let's get out of here – I'm buying you a drink right now,' he firmly said.

'But it's only 3 pm,' I protested. 'I have to get back to work or my boss will kill me.'

'Excuse me, I'm the client. I'm calling your boss to say I need you for a brainstorm. Think she'll argue with that?' he said authoritatively.

My tears dried instantly. God, masterful men are such a turn-on! Honestly, if Rahul were forty kg thinner at that moment, I'd have forgotten about that thin-skinned jerk Rehan.

The dimly lit bar Rahul took me to suited my mood. My only objection was that the table he'd chosen faced the wall.

'Let's sit there instead,' I pointed to a table at the centre of the room.

'No way, Diya,' he shuddered. 'If you start sobbing again, people will notice and think I was nasty to you.'

Gosh, Rahul was tops at strategy!

'Bloody Mary for you?' Rahul asked as a waiter hovered around us.

'Ew, no. You ruined it for me for life with that sanitary-napkin act,' I shuddered.

I ordered a G & T instead.

'Okay, how long have you known the creep?' he said after he'd placed an order for three plates of fish fingers, three plates of chicken tikka and three plates of shammi kebab along with our drinks.

'About ten days,' I mumbled.

Rahul raised his eyebrows so high they almost hit the ceiling. 'Bloody hell! Just ten effing days and you're crying like you're a character in a tragedy of epic proportions like *Dr Zhivago*?'

I snapped at him. 'Listen to the whole story – *my* tragic story, not a tragic story by some intense Russian – before judging me!'

Then I told him about the battle for Rehan between Anushka and me, and that night at home when he'd stormed out because of that innocent 'all-men-are-bastards' conversation.

'Humourless jerk,' Rahul muttered when I finished. 'And now he's dating some woman called Anushka and that's why you're really mad, right?'

'Yup,' I nodded.

'So let's put this on record: your feelings aren't hurt, but your ego is severely bruised.'

'The entire office thinks I'm a loser,' I whined piteously.

Rahul leaned forward conspiratorially. 'So here's how we fix him,' he began.

'Not just him,' I thumped the table. 'I want to fix her too!'

'Ah, in classic vengeful Hell's Angels mode,' Rahul chuckled, but when I glared at him he shut up and wiped the grin off his face.

'Sure, that can be arranged,' he said in a crisp, businesslike manner. 'Now listen up – my mum's boyfriend, er, sorry, my mum's boyfriend's son is a model and–'

I gaped.

'What? Your mum's sixty and she has a boyfriend?'

'Almost seventy,' he grinned. 'She lies about her age. But that's beside the point. See, Akhil is sexy. So sexy that sometimes when I'm with him, I wish I were gay.'

My eyes sparkled.

'Omigod, he's that scrumptious? When can I meet him?'

'He's out of the country for a week, at least,' Rahul shrugged.

'Oh no, I can't wait that long to fix them,' I wailed. 'Suppose Rehan gets seriously into Anushka before he returns?'

Rahul patted my arm in an avuncular manner.

'Despair not – we start fixing them tomorrow. I have an evil plan,' he chuckled.

Rahul's plan was simple: make the office (including Rehan and Anushka) believe that I was *not* a loser pining for Rehan.

'Rest assured Rehan will kick himself for dumping you after Project Akhil,' Rahul promised. 'Most men are dumb – if a super stud like Akhil pursues you, they find you more desirable.'

Rahul and I chatted on the phone all night, discussing the plan in minute detail, and I enjoyed myself thoroughly – so much that I forgot to check if Tanya was on Skype!

Mallika did pop into my room once to moan that 'That Rahul's phone is permanently engaged'. I put my finger on my lips and mouthed, 'Shh! I'm talking to him right now.'

She shook her head in a forlorn manner and shrugged.

'I give up. All he wants is you.'

I was too busy giggling at something Rahul had said to correct her. I mean, she was so far from the truth. Get real: if Rahul truly did want me, why would he help me get the man of my dreams?

And so, the very next day, a heart-shaped arrangement

of roses arrived at my office desk from Akhil. Well, from Rahul really, but it was signed 'Akhil'. It was so large and bizarre-looking, it got the office buzzing.

I called Rahul and hissed, 'It's working! But they want to know *everything* about him. What do I say?'

'Tell them you dated Akhil for ages but dumped him eventually because he wanted marriage and you weren't ready,' Rahul said smoothly.

On Day Two, a heart-shaped locket arrived with Akhil's photograph inside. Omigod, he was dreamy-looking. When I showed his photograph around, all the girls in office sighed.

Day Three was even more romantic: two guys arrived at my desk. One had a synthesizer and he started playing that UB40 song, 'Can't Help Falling in Love with You', while the other guy fixed me a cocktail. It had no umbrella but a cheesy heart-shaped swizzle stick to stir it with. The entire office crowd (including a sulky Rehan and a curious Anushka) was buzzing around my desk with excitement.

My boss, a hard-hearted Bitchzilla, blew her nose into a hanky and shouted, 'Say yes, Diya, godammit!' Almost everyone joined in the chorus and gosh, I felt like a rock star!

I called Rahul later and whispered, 'Darling,

you're terrific! Where did you find those guys?'

'Ve haf our vays,' he chuckled.

'So, what happens next?' I asked eagerly.

'Not telling you or you won't look surprised. But it's bloody bigger than today,' Rahul promised.

The icing on the cake was, later in the day, Rehan sent me an e-mail that simply said, 'Can we talk?'

Before I answered Rehan's 'Can we talk?' e-mail, I decided to call Rahul. After all, he was my personal strategy planner.

'Don't you dare reply!' Rahul barked.

'But why?' I argued. 'The objective was to make him come back and he clearly wants to.'

'If you're going to give in so fast, you're stupider than I imagined,' Rahul said with a pronounced sneer. 'Have some self-respect – make that guy sweat like a polar bear in the Sahara Desert in summer.'

'There are no polar bears in the Sahara Desert,' I pointed out in my best school-principal voice.

'You know what I mean,' Rahul said testily. 'Now follow the plan or I'm calling it quits!'

'Okay, whatever,' I said sulkily.

'Besides, I have one more surprise planned for tomorrow. Wait for that before you take any foolish decisions,' he ordered.

And boy oh boy, what a surprise that was! I was busy working at my desk when a deep voice said, 'It's lovely to see you again, Diya.'

I looked up and saw the incredibly sexy Akhil in person! And omigod, he looked even better than his photograph. My heart started racing like it was participating in an F1 race, and then I blacked out.

When I came to, I was lying on a sofa in the reception area. Now get this – my head was on Akhil's lap! Practically everyone in office was there, watching in amazement and envy. I can swear most of the women were drooling. Rehan was there as well, and he looked miserable and jealous!

'Feeling better now, darling?' Akhil said tenderly.

I nodded weakly and sat up.

'What you need is a shot of brandy and a long nap.' Akhil looked decisive.

Then he turned to the crowd and said, 'Is it okay if she leaves office for the day?'

'Yes! Yes! Yes!' everyone screamed excitedly, including my boss. Only Rehan remained silent.

Akhil lifted me in his arms and strode towards the elevator.

'I'm fine, I can walk,' I said shyly.

'Forget it,' Akhil hissed. 'Rahul gave me strict instructions to carry you out of the office like a rom-com hero. He said if I didn't he'd sit on me and squash me to pulp.'

By the time we got into the car, I wasn't in love with Rehan anymore. I was in lust with Akhil. Yes, I know I'm shallow and so what?

'So where are we going?' I peeped up at Akhil through my eyelashes and asked him coyly.

'For lunch as promised,' he said and reassuringly added, 'Rahul and my girlfriend are already there.'

'Oh great,' I said unenthusiastically. I mentally kicked myself for foolishly hoping that Akhil and I would have a cozy twosome, sparks would fly and our fake romance would become real. My only consolation was that Rehan's wounded expression had been priceless! He'd be putty in my hands after this.

As we entered the restaurant I spotted Rahul and his mum at a table in a far corner. My heart lifted – perhaps Akhil's girlfriend wouldn't show up and I'd have the opportunity to reel him in.

I was astonished when Akhil went up to Rahul's mum, kissed her on her lips and said, 'Mission accomplished, darling. Now, do you want to hang out with these kids or should we do our own thing?'

Rahul's mum smiled sunnily at me. She was still so attractive, even her crow's feet looked dead sexy.

'First, a toast to my clever son,' she said, and I

noticed that a bottle of champagne was chilling in a bucket.

'To the best son in the world,' she said, raising her glass.

'To the most devious bastard in the world,' Akhil said.

I raised my glass and the words that tripped out of my mouth surprised me.

'To my second-best friend in the world,' I said with true warmth. I had finally found someone quite as cozy to be with as Tanya!

'For the record, I don't like being second best,' Rahul growled.

'Deal with it!' I shrugged, and his mum giggled.

After Akhil and his mum left, I asked Rahul why he'd lied to me.

'About what?' he looked genuinely surprised.

'You said Akhil was her boyfriend's son,' I admonished him.

'Oh, that! Yeah, well, that's because not too many people get their relationship,' he said in his defence. 'She's almost twice his age, and people act like it's odd and amusing and get bitchy about it. The problem with this country is that most people are mentally provincial.' He sniffed contemptuously when he said that.

I scrunched my brow.

'To hell with what other people think. I'm very clear that I have just one life to live and I'm going to do it my way,' I said defiantly.

'Exactly. Akhil makes her happy and that's what I want for my mum.'

'And what makes *you* happy, Rahul, apart from food, of course?' I teased.

'You,' he said and looked me in the eye.

Then he leaned back in his chair and gazed at me like I was his favourite daughter or something. 'See, I like being with you. You're a bitch and refreshingly honest about being a bitch. I hate fakes.'

I felt flattered. More flattered than if he'd just told me that my eyes were like melting pools blah blah blah.

My phone beeped suddenly. It was a text message from Rehan, begging to take me out to dinner. I punched in a yes and then told Rahul.

His face darkened.

'Dammit Diya, don't tell me you still want to go out with that creep?' he frowned.

I looked at him, puzzled.

'Hello, that was our plan, wasn't it? To get him interested in me?'

Rahul shook his head slowly.

'Not really,' he said ruefully. 'My plan was to help

you see him for the twerp he is. See how easily manipulated he was? He didn't want you when he could have had you – but he wanted you when someone else wanted you. Could you really have a relationship with a wimpy, shallow person?'

I sprang to Rehan's defence in a trice. 'Hey, I'm shallow too,' I pointed out. 'Which is why Rehan and I will be perfect for each other,' I added rather vehemently.

Rahul astonished me by putting his hand over mine.

'Don't do it, Diya – please don't meet him,' he said urgently.

His eyes, however, said something else. They begged, 'Take me, not him!'

Impossible! I scraped my chair back and got up.

'Listen Rahul, I'm being a refreshingly honest bitch now and saying nothing can ever happen between us apart from friendship, okay?' I said firmly.

'Is it because I'm overweight?' Rahul asked in a low voice.

I didn't answer. I just walked away without looking back.

I was on a crazy high the next month.

1. I got my man! And he was amazingly loving and attentive – all the more so because I had helped put him on a higher pedestal at the office by supposedly dumping the scrumptious Akhil for him. He owed me big time!
2. Anushka got her comeuppance, hurrah! She was slinking around the office looking like a wounded jackass.
3. Tanya was finally on Skype!
4. Mavis informed me that the top-management types who had initially lost their bet on Rehan asking me out on a date first had had another bet that Rehan would eventually dump Anushka for me, and they finally won. Bigger money was at stake, apparently! I got so many friendly smiles that I was emboldened enough to ask to be taken off the sanitary-napkin account. I couldn't bear the idea of interacting with Rahul again. I felt hugely embarrassed that he was in love with me – and guilty that I couldn't reciprocate it.

Just when I thought that nothing, absolutely nothing, could rain on my parade, Mallika did. We were chatting late one night after I got back from a date with Rehan, and she was whining about the fact that she still hadn't met an interesting man.

'Call Rahul, then,' I told her excitedly. 'You used to have a crush on him so why don't you follow it up?'

She wrinkled her nose.

'Not yet. You just broke his heart; I think it's prudent to give him a few months to recover first.'

I felt terribly guilty then.

'Look, I never asked him to fall in love with me. I never led him up the garden path or anything slimy like that,' I said in my defence.

'Yeah, I know that, but I still feel bad for him. He's such a nice guy,' Mallika sighed.

'He is, isn't he? He's fabulously witty too,' I admitted.

'And under all those layers of adipose tissue there's a very, very sexy man who refuses to get out. Way sexier than your Rehan. I mean, Rahul's dimples, gosh, they turn my knees to jelly,' Mallika sighed again.

'Hmm. I've always told Rahul that he'll be seriously attractive if he stops stuffing his face with food,' I agreed.

'That's it. I'm going to call him first thing tomorrow and I'm definitely going to get him!' Mallika said decisively. I felt a twinge of jealousy when she said that. Just a twinge, mind you.

When I went to bed later, I found myself thinking of Rahul's dimples instead of Rehan's flat abs. And his sense of humour. And the fact that he enjoyed me for who I was, warts and all. I had to get Rahul back as a friend again, I just had to!

The next evening I asked Mallika if she'd called him. She pulled a face.

'Well, I called all day, every hour on the hour, but his phone was switched off.'

'Maybe he's in a conference or something tedious,' I yawned and kicked off my shoes.

'I haven't finished,' Mallika said, looking slightly bashful. 'I did my usual desperado act – I called his office and was informed that he was transferred to Bangalore a couple of weeks ago. So there go my dreams of Rahul. I'm moving on.'

'Bangalore?' I squawked. 'I had no idea!'

I began to feel as glum as Mallika was looking. I suddenly missed him!

I hugged her hard and she hugged me back. God, if Rahul was even aware that two women were pining for him, his jaw would probably drop to his knees! I couldn't stop smiling at the thought.

I left office very early the next day. My head was hurting because Rehan had invited me home to meet his mother next week. He'd issued the invitation like he was doing me a favour – the cheek!

After brooding over Rehan's meet-the-mother invitation, I had a chat with a very sleepy Tanya on Skype. I had called her and ordered her to get online ASAP.

'This had better be an earth-shattering crisis, Diya, or I'll murder you for waking me up at such an ungodly hour,' Tanya grumbled.

'It *is* earth-shattering,' I moaned. 'Rehan wants me to meet his beloved mum. Which, as we both know, means he thinks I'm seriously into him! Horrible, horrible, horrible – men really are stupid. Help me dump him!'

'You woke me up for this?' Tanya shrieked.

'Hey, you're my best friend! I can wake you up at 3 am even if I want to know if purple is the new black,' I chided.

'Damn you, Diya, may you rot in hell,' Tanya snarled.

I stuck out my tongue at her.

'Skip the profanities and start the counselling like you always do,' I pleaded. 'My head hurts so,' I whimpered, appealing to her softer side.

Tanya relented. She dished out brutal home truths. Like how I never stuck with a man more than a few months because I always chose people who were completely wrong for me and inevitably I got bored and ran away.

I did what I usually do – I blamed my divorced parents for it. 'Look, Tanya, my parents taught me that there's no such thing as true love, okay?'

'Rot!' she scoffed. 'They may not have found true love with each other, but they both found other partners they're deliriously happy with.'

'Well, maybe,' I grudgingly conceded.

'Why can't you just be friends with a guy first, you ass? If you like him, then take the relationship further. All this rushing in and rushing out that you do is the silliest thing ever,' Tanya scolded. She was in full spate now.

'Hold it right there, Tanya – I've got something to say to you,' I beseeched. I told her all about Rahul. How much I liked him and how fat he was and how silly I'd been. She'd missed out on the Rahul part of my life because she got onto Skype only after I'd started dating Rehan.

Tanya was silent for long after I finished relating the Rahul episode. And then she started laughing.

'What's so funny?' I demanded.

'You! You're so funny! I mean, how can you let a few kilos come between you and a potentially deep and meaningful relationship?'

'It's not a few kilos, it's well over forty!' I said crossly.

'Big deal!' Tanya snorted.

My phone rang midway through the conversation. Tanya raised her eyebrows as she heard me tell Rehan I couldn't meet him that night. And she started grinning like the Cheshire cat in *Alice in Wonderland* when I told him, 'Why don't you ask Anushka to join you tonight instead? The poor thing was dumped recently, she could do with some cheering up.'

'You are an absolute bitch and I love you for it,' Tanya blew me a kiss.

'Funnily enough, Rahul said almost the same thing to me,' I sighed deeply.

'Hell, just a few kilos,' Tanya said musingly.

'Over forty!' I reminded her indignantly.

'Well, do what you think is best then. Nighty-night,' Tanya cooed and hastily went offline before I could say a word.

I thought about it all night. It was nearing dawn when I had my epiphany: if Tanya had been a man, I'd have married her whether she was thin or fat or tall or short or paralysed waist down. I just wanted to be with her because she got me. And there was another person out there who got me too and all I needed to do was get him as well. Literally.

I took an early morning flight to Bangalore. But before I left the flat, I hastily scribbled a semi-apologetic note for Mallika that said, 'Since you've decided to move on from Rahul, would it be okay if I moved in with him?' It was a purely rhetorical question, of course.

When I strode into Rahul's office, the receptionist tried to call him but I stopped her with an urgent whisper, 'Please don't call him. Look, I'm his fiancée from Mumbai and this is a surprise visit.'

It wasn't really a lie. I was certain I would walk out as his fiancée. Well, not dead certain, but I kind of hoped.

Her eyes became round, and she led me to his room with a conspiratorial smile.

I knocked tentatively and my pulse raced when he said, 'Come in.' God, how I'd missed that voice.

'What the fuck are you doing here?' Rahul looked up with a start as I walked in with a wide smile.

'It's lovely to see you too, darling,' I said.

His eyes scanned my face and then he said with a sneer, 'So Rehan dumped you again?'

'Nope. I fell in love with someone else,' I said cheerfully.

'And you've come to me for advice? Is that why you're here?' He shook his head and muttered incoherently.

'Nope, I've got a wedding invitation for you,' I said as I hoisted a two-kg chocolate cake out of my tote bag. 'It's an edible invite; I got it specially made for you.' I lifted the cardboard lid and placed the cake box under his nose. The icing said, 'Will you marry me, you big fat fool?'

Rahul looked taken aback.

'What, cat got your tongue?' I enquired sweetly.

He grinned, 'No, a bitch got it instead.'

'So is it a big fat yes then?' I asked. I sounded cool but I was a little anxious.

'Nope, it's a big fat maybe,' he said and looked a little stern.

After he ate the cake, though, he said 90 per cent yes. I knew he would, because it was a deadly delicious chocolate truffle.

'Heck, I thought you'd be thin and gaunt pining for me but I see that you've put on another five kg at least,' I said conversationally as I parked myself on his comfy lap.

'Comfort food,' he shrugged. 'You drove me to it!'

Later, when he took me to a restaurant and placed an

order for three dum biryanis, I put my foot down.

'Change the order to just one dum biryani, please,' I told the waiter firmly.

Rahul looked mildly surprised.

'You're not eating, is it?'

'Of course I am! We're sharing it, that's all.'

'Just one between the two of us?' he whined.

'Yes, this is what sharing lives is all about, you big fat fool,' I said with my newly acquired worldly wisdom.

'Dammit! I absolutely refuse to marry you in that case!' he said and stamped his foot like a petulant child. The table shook.

'Sorry, I do not accept rejection,' I told him calmly and then launched into a speech I'd prepared in my head on the flight.

'You're about forty kg overweight. I find that unacceptable, but I'm willing to meet you halfway. Which means you knock off twenty kg whether you like it or not.'

'Or not!' Rahul thundered.

I changed tack then and squeezed my eyes shut really tight to induce tears.

'This is so not fair, Rahul,' I said in a weepy voice. 'You're willing to give me your heart, but you want me to take clogged arteries with it too. Perhaps you're right, we shouldn't get married or I'll be a widow before I'm twenty-eight years old!'

Rahul looked guilt-stricken.

'Okay, okay,' he mumbled, 'we'll share one damn dum biryani if that makes you happy.'

'It makes me *very* happy!' I said cheerfully.

I wasn't that mean to him, though. I gave him most of the dum biryani and made him chew it very slowly.

'Make sure each bite stays in your mouth for at least five minutes,' I warned him.

I nodded approvingly as the poor chap chewed slowly, and reached out to squeeze his hand affectionately.

'I'm spending the night with you, if you don't mind,' I said.

Rahul's eyes gleamed. He pushed his half-eaten plate away and signalled to the waiter for the bill.

'Only to make sure you don't raid the fridge at midnight,' I grinned at him.

Rahul laughed and shook his head ruefully.

'Bloody Hell's Angel,' he muttered and snatched his plate back from the astonished waiter.

2

Love in F Major

'He looks tense. Do you think he's going to tell her tonight?' Ravi said. Joaquin glanced in the direction of the young couple whose drinks he was mixing and shook his head.

'I doubt it. Besides, she's doing all the talking – how can he get a word in edgewise? Women are terrible creatures, they talk, talk, talk all the time.'

Ravi looked disappointed. It had been over a month since he had witnessed a dramatic break-up at the pub. The girl had poured a bottle of tomato ketchup on the boy's head and then flung a plate of piping hot cocktail sausages at him for good measure. Great fun!

He served Jayant and Nasreen their drinks and lingered a little longer at their table, fiddling with the ice bucket and rearranging the coasters, trying to catch what Nasreen was saying. It was just some rubbish about her office. Something about someone called Atul congratulating her on an assignment and asking her out for a drink to celebrate.

'I told him I had other plans. He's such a dirty old man,' Nasreen made a face. 'He actually told me to go home and slip into something sexy and that he'd pick me up at nine-ish. And would you believe that he has an impossibly gorgeous wife and two cute children? Their photographs are plastered on practically every inch of his cabin walls and yet the shameless man makes a pass at anything in a skirt.'

Jayant merely grunted and Nasreen carried on.

'I asked Atul if I'm going to get a raise and a promotion for getting new business and he was suddenly several degrees less enthusiastic. He said he'll consider it when my appraisal comes up next March, the liar! And then he patted my hand in a decidedly non-avuncular manner, ew.'

Ravi drifted away from Nasreen's dull conversation. If he'd stayed a second longer he'd have fallen asleep on his feet. On his way back to the bar, a regular who gave him unusually generous tips tapped him on the shoulder and asked him to make the music louder. He readily complied with a warm smile.

The DJ was playing such fantastic retro music that Nasreen didn't want to step outside for a smoke but Jayant insisted.

'After this song,' she pouted and Jayant scowled.

'Why are you making that face? God, I had no idea irritable bowel syndrome could actually make people irritable,' she teased.

'What? This blasted music is so loud I can't hear you!' Jayant shouted.

'I said, I had no idea that your irritable bowel syndrome thingie could make you so irritable,' Nasreen screamed.

Jayant heard her loud and clear. And, evidently, so did other people up to three tables away from them. They looked vastly amused.

Jayant got up abruptly and left. Nasreen caught sight of his thunderous expression and dashed off at his heels. Ravi didn't bother to scurry after them in a panic. They were regulars, they'd be back to pay the bill.

After about half an hour, Nasreen slunk back in alone and ordered a Long Island Iced Tea. Ravi nodded and went to the bar.

'What? She's had three large vodkas already – we'll have to carry her out,' Joaquin muttered disapprovingly.

'Look at her face. He must have just told her about that other pretty woman he brings here occasionally – see, I told you I had a feeling he'd tell her tonight,' Ravi said with a snigger as he loaded his tray with the stale salted peanuts they served as freebies.

Nasreen had never bothered to pay attention to the lyrics of 'Come Undone' before – she'd just enjoyed the music. That night, though, she caught a few of the words and soulfully felt that the song was written specially for her.

'Who do you need, who do you love/When you come undone?' Simon Le Bon of Duran Duran wailed and Nasreen wailed along with him.

She didn't have to be carried to a taxi, much to the bartender's relief. Another man joined her soon after. He looked old enough to be her dad, perhaps he *was* her dad, Joaquin mused.

'Nah,' Ravi said dismissively. 'She called him by his name. Atul or something like that. And she wants another Long Island Iced Tea. A single malt on the rocks for him. Large. '

By the end of the evening, when the DJ was playing Pink Floyd's 'Coming Back to Life', his standard goodnight-and-get-out-before-the-cops-rush-in-and-fine-us song, Nasreen was unabashedly sitting on the man's lap and sobbing into his left shoulder. The damp patch on his shirt was growing by the second. If she didn't stop soon, it would spread to another continent.

'Perhaps you're right,' Ravi grudgingly conceded. 'It probably *is* her dad.'

Joaquin grinned triumphantly.

The morning after, Nasreen solemnly contemplated the eleventh glass of chilled water she was drinking. *That Rhonda Byrne woman who wrote that crappy positive thinking book,* The Secret, *would probably rap me on the knuckles for saying this, but I swear, whichever way I look at my glass, it seems half-empty.*

She flung herself on the bed and let the tears flow unchecked. She even allowed herself to howl loudly like a wolf on a full moon night. And cursed herself for not listening to her friends when Jayant had proposed a year ago.

'What's wrong with you, Nasreen? He's not a stranger. Come on, you guys have been seeing each other for, like, three years!' Ritu had screeched.

'I'm not saying no, I'm merely saying not yet. Oh god, you married types are such a pain,' Nasreen had complained. 'Your mission in life is not to save the planet or hug trees – nothing as noble as that. Your energies are completely focused on persuading me to settle down. The cheek, considering that all of you are always moaning about how deathly dull your boyfriends have become after marriage. "He doesn't want to go to restaurants any more, leave alone pubs. All he does is watch mindless rubbish on TV."' Nasreen mimicked her friends and then added sternly, 'If marriage sucks, why insist that I do it? I thought we were friends, not enemies!'

'Misery loves company,' they had shamelessly said with wide grins. 'And, besides, Jayant and you are so good together.'

Yes, we were good together till he started seeing someone else, Nasreen thought bitterly and howled even louder. She now sounded like a chorus of three anguished wolves with thorns in their paws baying at the moon.

Her cell phone rang and Nasreen picked it up, glancing anxiously at the caller identity. She hoped it was Jayant saying that he'd made a mistake and was sorry and could they get back together, please?

It *was* Jayant. But he was saying something that she hadn't scripted in her head.

'Give my turntable and LPs to Rajat – I'll collect them from him later,' Jayant said tersely.

'Look, can we talk?' Nasreen begged.

'It really is over, Nas. There's nothing left to say,' Jayant said gently, so gently that Nasreen knew for sure that it was over. Jayant disconnected the call.

The phone rang again a second later. Nasreen snatched it eagerly, hoping that Jayant had had a sudden change of heart. The caller identity said Atul. She flung the phone down, unanswered.

That damn Atul has no reason to call, she thought uncharitably. *I mean, he was the one who told me to take the day off from work last night.*

A few hours later, the doorbell rang. Nasreen leapt up to answer it, mopping her tears with her tee as she raced to the door, praying that it would be Jayant.

It was Atul. He had a bunch of flowers in one hand and two bottles of wine in the other.

'Look, I really need to be alone,' Nasreen said firmly and then burst into tears.

Ten minutes later, she sighed appreciatively, 'Hmm, nice wine.'

A couple of hours later she protested, 'Hands off! I mean, you could well have been to school with my dad. You may even have played marbles with him, for all I know.'

But then she remembered that Jayant was probably in the throes of passion with his latest girlfriend, and she was possibly being very, very, very good to him because he had chosen her over Nasreen.

Why should I be celibate when he's absolutely, positively, definitely celebrating? Nasreen thought bitterly.

A little later, Nasreen moaned. 'Gosh, why

didn't someone, anyone tell me about older men before?'

The next morning, Nasreen woke up feeling new. She'd finally realized why she'd been unable to weep with gratitude when Jayant had proposed to her earlier: the missing link had been discovered! She had completely gotten over him overnight, without listening to inspiring make-the-creep-weep songs like Lily Allen's 'Smile' or Pink's 'So What' on a loop.

That's how it began with Atul. Not exactly Romeo-and-Juliet stuff, but it worked.

In all fairness, he did treat her better than any man ever had (apart from her dad, of course). Besides, he was so mature, he made Jayant seem like a retard. Take an Audi, for example. Jayant would let out an exaggerated sigh if ever he saw one parked on the road and would examine it keenly from all angles, quite like an amorous tiger circling a tigress during the mating season. Sometimes he'd go down on all fours for a closer look at the chassis and once Nasreen was sure that she'd caught him sniffing it, though Jayant hotly denied it. On that very same occasion, the owner slid into the car while Jayant was admiring it and revved the engine. The low growl it emitted sounded pretty much like a tiger in heat, to Nasreen's amusement.

'You should be on Nat Geo,' Nasreen had told Jayant, who continued to stare longingly at the rear of the speeding car till it became a speck in the distance.

Jayant had scowled.

Atul never did that. He *owned* a goddamned Audi. And Atul was a good-looking dude too. Middle-aged, admittedly, but not short and bald with a beer belly.

At the beginning, Nasreen never asked Atul to leave his wife. She didn't even care. As far as she was concerned, he was her transition man. Nasreen's friends were not as complacent as she was, though. They would shake their heads and sigh, 'Have you thought about the pain you're putting his family through?'

'Hah!' Nasreen would snort defiantly. 'I'm not putting them through pain – *he* is. I'm not cheating on anyone – *he* is. I can't understand why women who discover that their husbands are having an affair blame the other woman. Some even rush to their homes or offices and scream and shout and kick them in public. They're just in denial. They should physically assault their lying, cheating husbands instead, isn't it? If Atul's wife ever comes for me with a sharpened steak knife, I'll tell her the whole truth: her husband shamelessly pursued me. Face it, I'm not a vamp, I'm a victim. Hell, I'm as much a victim as she is.' She'd look her friends in the eye when she made her fiery speech, because she really did believe it.

Nasreen's friends would nod slowly in agreement, but still look uncomfortable.

'Even so,' Ritu had said reasonably, 'it's easier for you to walk out than it is for his wife, what with the kids and all.' She'd looked at Nasreen with hope shining in her eyes.

'I *will* walk out as soon as I meet someone nice. After all, Atul's just my transition man,' Nasreen had snapped. Then she sighed deeply. 'Like that matters, though. My walking out will make no difference to his poor wife. He'll replace me with someone else pronto, that's what he'll do. Only when he's ninety and incapable of running after women will she get him to herself. I bet she knows that already. And if the silly woman is willing to wait it out, that's her problem!'

And then one of Nasreen's friends would helpfully switch to a more innocuous subject like the latest diet fad or the ignominy of childbirth and Nasreen would stop feeling like a hunted animal.

What she never did tell her friends was that, in

the recent past, Atul's wife had popped into office to pick him up. She'd made it a point to stop by at Nasreen's desk to say hello. While her smile hadn't quite been genuine, she hadn't looked at Nasreen with loathing. Instead, there had been a silent but urgent plea in her eyes that gave Nasreen insomnia till she discovered the joy of sleeping tablets.

Soon, the entire office got wind of the affair. It was the hottest topic on the gossip charts, shoving the junior art director who stole office laptops and cameras to fund his cocaine habit to second place. Senior management snobs were politer to Nasreen than they'd ever been – she was the woman their branch head was wooing, after all. On the flip side, the office peons treated Nasreen more insolently than before – she'd catch them exchanging smirks when she was around. Sometimes she'd have to bite her tongue to stop herself from launching into her standard 'I'm not a vamp, I'm a victim' speech but she thought it best not to publicly admit to her affair. Besides, she had no idea what the words for 'vamp' and 'victim' were in Marathi and couldn't be bothered to find out.

Life was bearable till jealousy tripped Nasreen and she accidentally fell in love with her transition man.

She could deal with Atul spending weekends with his family, and at office parties when he studiously ignored her because his wife was playing gracious hostess at his side. However, a week-long beach holiday with his family in Thailand gave her the worst acidity attack she'd ever had in her life. It began with his 'Wish you were here' text message. 'I hope there's a tsunami,' she'd viciously replied and she'd meant it. Ten minutes later, she started worrying about whether there really would be a tsunami and how desolate her life would be without Atul. Nasreen checked the weather report in Thailand on the Internet every single day till Atul got back as brown as multigrain toast. That's when she discovered that it wouldn't be easy to call it quits.

The tears began when photographs of the Thailand holiday went up on his cabin walls. Nasreen experienced an overpowering urge to buy darts and perfect her aim in his cabin.

She'd asked Atul once, in what she'd thought was an arch manner, 'Am I just a toy girl to you?'

He'd laughed, 'Ah, toy girl – I like that. You're my very own Barbie!'

'Ew! I *hate* Barbie,' Nasreen had protested angrily. 'And I don't even have knockers like her, so there!'

He'd just laughed some more and Nasreen's hopes of the conversation leading to a meaningful discussion on their future together were dashed.

Nasreen's nights out with the girls gradually became more depressing than fun because she'd wonder what Atul was doing or, rather, *who* Atul was doing while she was away. She'd started whining to her friends, 'What almost kills me is the fact that he never ever mentions that we have a future together as a legitimate couple. I get flowers and chocolate instead. Those I can buy for myself, thank you very much!'

Nasreen's friends found her repetitive conversation hugely boring after a while. It was painfully evident that she'd reached a dead end in the relationship. They starting urging her to give Atul an ultimatum: 'Do it now while you're still thirty-one, before you have wrinkles,' they hissed. 'Men don't leave their wives for women who look like their grandmothers!'

Nasreen had had enough of her hopeless situation too – she couldn't get the picture of him sharing a bed with his wife out of her head, despite the fact that he swore they never made out.

She delivered the ultimatum eventually, valiantly quelling her fear that he'd abruptly walk out: 'Me or her? Choose.'

Atul had glared at her and then sighed wearily. 'Oh, good heavens. Give me a week,' he'd muttered, and walked out of her flat. Nasreen ordered a twelve-inch pizza for dinner to fill up the emptiness in her life. She ate it all, every scrap, and still felt unfulfilled.

Atul avoided Nasreen for the next six days – it was not difficult because he was the boss and could lock himself in his cabin all day if he wished, playing Spider Solitaire or Angry Birds. She was swallowing antacids by the handful – and would get particularly nasty heartburn attacks when female colleagues would enter his cabin for meetings and exit giggling at some flirtatious remark he may have or, rather, *must* have made. Just when Nasreen had forlornly assumed that he had already made the decision to ignore her forever, on D-day he came up to her after work and grimly said, 'You ready to leave?'

Both of them were silent during the drive to Nasreen's flat. Her stomach was tied up in knots till Atul parked the car outside her building, opened the dicky and took out a suitcase. It didn't look large enough for a lifetime or even a week together, Nasreen noted with disappointment, but she didn't bring it up until they were cozily sharing her armchair. Atul made it clear that this was just a trial, while his family was away on a month-long holiday. If it worked, then he'd file for divorce.

'Right, now first things first,' Atul said, raking his fingers through his hair.

Nasreen grinned and started unbuttoning his shirt, but Atul gently pushed her away.

'Not now, young lady. I want you to go to your building society office and book a parking space for my car right away. I refuse to leave it outside the building. And make sure I get stilt parking, okay?'

'That can wait till tomorrow,' Nasreen groaned.

'No, it can't,' Atul said firmly. 'It's not an ordinary car, for heaven's sake – it's a goddamned Audi!'

Heck, he said 'Audi' in the same awe-struck tones as Jayant did, Nasreen thought with dismay.

That was, perhaps, the most wonderful night in Nasreen's life. Despite the fact that Atul smelt different in his pyjamas. The seductive musky scent of the aftershave he used during the day was showered away and replaced with a strong, sharp eucalyptus scent.

'Chest congestion,' he'd said with a hint of embarrassment as he placed a tiny bottle of decongestant cream on Nasreen's bedside table.

Nasreen didn't have strong objections to the

eucalyptus cream since it brought back fond memories of her ailing grandmother – not sexy, but she could just about manage to live with it. She didn't even flinch a few days later when Atul asked her to help him tweeze the hair growing on his ear lobes (now that was a turn-off, but she did it anyway), but what she couldn't deal with was his obsession with food. He was shocked that Nasreen's fridge was as bare as old Mother Hubbard's cupboard. He thought it ridiculous that all her meals were from takeaway joints and lectured her severely on it. It was like living with her mother! And it bored her to tears when he started reminiscing about freshly squeezed orange juice, filter coffee, roast chicken with baby potatoes and suchlike that his wife would lovingly stuff his face with! She was reminded of a silly Red Riding Hood cartoon she'd seen in an adult magazine, where the heroine is seriously annoyed with the Big Bad Wolf and screams, 'Food, food, food – doesn't anyone want sex any more?'

But, god knows, she tried. She'd surprised him with a bacon and eggs fry-up for breakfast one morning but instead of kissing her feet with gratitude, Atul had shoved the plate away and settled for toast instead.

'High cholesterol,' he'd said in a flat voice.

Their big fight happened over the television on Day Seven. To Nasreen's horror, every night Atul would watch news channels on a loop. And he lost it when Nasreen considerately suggested that perhaps he needed memory tablets, since he'd forgotten the news he'd just heard ten minutes ago. *Jayant preferred music and entertainment channels like me*, Nasreen thought glumly. She didn't say it aloud, though, for fear that it would add fuel to an already blazing fire.

Being together just wasn't fun any more. That's when Nasreen learnt a universal truth: living in is not as thrilling as dating. No more flowers and chocolate, only arguments over silly things. It was different with Jayant, she thought wistfully, but perhaps it was because they just spent weekends together and had similar interests, as well. They both enjoyed takeaway meals, for starters!

On the ninth night, Atul tore himself away from a news channel and said they had to talk. *What does he want to crib about now*, Nasreen sighed inwardly. *Have we run out of cuff-and-collar cleaner for his precious shirts? Does he need laxatives or antacids? Am I going to get a lecture for leaving crumbs on the bed? Is he going to whine nostalgically about the boneless pepper chicken and brown rice that his wife cooks for dinner every Friday no matter what – even if an airplane slams into their apartment?*

'I'm sorry, I can't do this. My wife and children will be devastated if I leave them,' he had said in a sombre voice. His eyes were glued to the floor.

Nasreen pondered deeply over his statement for a few minutes, then softly but firmly said, 'Then you should go. You *must* go. Go now!' She felt noble. She felt proud. But most of all, she felt relieved. Hugely relieved.

Atul tried to look mournful when he opened the front door, and lingered there with his suitcase in a gloomy manner. 'I'm sorry, I tried,' he said in a low voice. Nasreen shrugged and shut the door hastily – she had to do it fast before he launched into that rubbishy 'We can still be friends' lie that men of all ages trot out. She could swear she heard him whistling a cheerful tune while waiting for the lift to arrive. It was probably some jazzy number from a 1950s musical, she thought with a smirk.

The second Nasreen heard the lift door slam shut, she raced to the bedroom and flung herself on the bed, exulting in the fact that she didn't have to share it with anyone any more. She leapt up a split second later to change the bed-sheets – they were reeking of eucalyptus.

'Guess who's here after so many months?' Ravi

excitedly told Joaquin who looked up and gave a low whistle.

'Oooh, this will be fun, considering that Jayant is here too with his pretty girlfriend.'

'She wants a Bloody Mary tonight – do you think she'll pour it over his head?' Ravi rubbed his hands with glee.

'In that case, I'll add extra Tabasco and pepper so that it stings his eyes,' Joaquin chuckled.

Ravi and Joaquin were sorely disappointed, though. Nasreen didn't bother to even glance in Jayant's direction. She was singing along to the music with her girlfriends, enjoying her freedom.

'One would think they were strangers,' Ravi said with disgust.

'These modern girls,' Joaquin wrinkled his nose like there was a dead rat in the room.

3

Welcome to the Sisterhood

If a weatherman had been asked to describe Antara's personality, he'd have smiled indulgently and said, 'Mainly sunny with blue skies'. Freak cyclones are difficult to predict, after all. And when one suddenly whooshed into Antara's life and turned the world as she knew it upside down, she felt like her soul had been slaughtered. With no one to turn to for sympathy, she poured out her anguish on her new blog, http://cruellycrushedlikeacockroach.blogspot.in. Like Kafka, she had got in touch with her dark side.

Antara's crisis would, admittedly, have been easier to deal with if Ajay had ruthlessly dumped her for another woman. After several crying bouts she could have worked up a formidable amount of rage against him and burnt his photographs, et cetera. But it wasn't quite like that. She couldn't hate him. In fact, she'd hate herself if she hated him. What she could do, though, was persuade Ajay to change his mind. Using logic this time instead of tears.

She put up a good fight.

'Men have it better than women do,' Antara said sagely to Ajay. 'You never have to pour boiling hot wax over your limbs to de-fuzz them. You never have to suffer god-awful cramps and practically bleed to death every month because you don't have periods. You don't have to risk catching creepy, socially embarrassing infections in public loos because you can pee standing up. And, never ever forget this,' Antara paused dramatically before delivering the last but most important advantage, in her opinion: 'if you have a one-night stand you're flatteringly labelled a stud, not a slut. So why on earth do you want to have this sex change operation thingie and become a woman?' A hint of frustration had crept into her voice.

Ajay shrugged. 'Maybe because I really am a woman? Didn't you ever suspect I was sort of girlie? Or, well, you might have thought I was gay-ish?'

Antara scrunched her brow. 'Hmm, I guess the time you leapt on a chair when there was a rat in the room, I kind of wondered,' she said flippantly. The fact was, she'd been so lost in her Ajay's-*the*-one-for-me fantasy, she'd never really noticed.

'Not even the time I refused to make out with you?' Ajay raised an eyebrow.

'Nope,' Antara shrugged. 'I just thought you were too smashed to play dildo. Didn't suspect. After all, you're a rugby player.' She gazed into space for a while. 'Okay, so when I caught you kissing that weedy boy behind the college canteen you were making out, not teaching him how to give tongue like you said?'

'Bingo, bimbo! And, might I add, he wasn't weedy, he was bloody hot!' Ajay sighed reminiscently.

Antara tried hard to suppress a feeling of revulsion. It never is easy when the man you've spent years fantasizing about confesses that he'd like to wear G-strings too. She hurriedly quelled the thought and asked, 'So when are you telling your parents?'

Ajay sank into gloom.

'Tonight, if Dad is in a good mood after he knocks back his fifth drink. And Mum is so relieved he hasn't used her as a punching bag that she'll agree to any bloody thing. Even if I tell her I'm giving up my respectable job at the bank to become a plumber.'

'Reason No. 5 not to become a woman!' Antara crowed triumphantly. 'You've never heard of husband-beating, have you?'

Ajay ruffled her hair affectionately. 'Hey, don't worry. I'll take martial arts classes soon after the sex change. I keep telling Mum to do that or to call the cops but she refuses.'

'Either she's in constant touch with her inner doormat or she foolishly thinks that if a woman allows her husband to beat her, she'll attain nirvana in this life,' Antara offered, glad that they'd switched the subject. She made a determined attempt to keep her voice normal.

Ajay looked contemplative. 'Well, you're probably right about that pious shit. I swear, every morning Mum scatters stale chapatis for the birds on the veranda just in case God is watching and giving her marks. Then she spends the rest of the day shooing them away for crapping on her precious potted plants. Does your mum think the same way too?'

Antara shook her head emphatically. 'No way. She's not remotely in touch with God or her inner doormat. I doubt she even has an inner doormat! She'd beat my dad to a pulp if he even dared to raise his voice against her. She's India's closet Lorena Bobbitt – you know, that woman who cut off her husband's penis in a fit of rage. They're probably twins separated at birth.'

Her bra strap slid from under her sleeveless tee and Ajay was mesmerized. He felt an overpowering urge to run a finger against the deliciously cool satin smoothness of the fabric but held back. Antara would pass out in horror. He could tell that his confession had made her queasy. He wondered if he should have told her at all, then decided he was glad he had. Hell, she was his best friend! He didn't want to lose her after he was qualified to exchange horror stories on men. And, all things considered, she'd taken it rather well. Oh, there was that sickening moment when he saw betrayal in her eyes. He'd known for years that she was in love with him, and it hurt him to hurt her.

On an impulse he hugged her. 'Just want you to know that if I were a man, you'd be my main squeeze. There's no one in the world I love more.' As Antara buried her face into his chest, a stray thought entered her head that the next time she snuggled up she'd encounter squishy twin peaks. She hastily disentangled herself, and wished she had an air-sickness bag handy. *Note to self*, her brain muttered, *pinch several barf bags from the seat pocket the next time you fly.*

Ajay sensed her distaste and got up, dusting soggy crumbs of chips off his clothes. He'd give her some time to deal with this. God knows it wasn't easy for him either, despite the fact that he'd been tossing the idea around in his head for years.

Antara followed him to the door and attempted to lighten the atmosphere.

'I'll teach you how to use make-up when you, um …'

Ajay wheeled around and raised a scornful eyebrow: '*You'll* teach me? Forget it babe, I'll bloody teach you. I'm far, far better at it than you! Hello, I've been practising every night for years. And guess what, sweetie, you still don't know your foundation shade.'

Antara's hands flew to her hips. 'And *you* know something, my precious flower? You're almost there without this operation. Honestly, you're a total bitch!'

Ajay grinned. He stretched out his arms for a hug, and this time Antara clung to him like a limpet. He drew her closer, tighter to him as he felt hot tears scald his t-shirt.

His body stiffened, though, when Antrara made her final muffled plea.

'Dammit Ajay, you can always cross-dress in fishnet stockings and stuff socks in your bra when the mood takes you. Why do you want to make it irreversible? Why do you want to become a bloody freak?'

He abruptly pushed her away.

'You ass, I don't want to be a bloody freak either –

that's what I currently am! I want to be normal. Just a normal girl like you! That,' he continued bitterly, 'is what Mother Nature originally intended for me, and midway through, shc possibly got distracted by a tornado or something terribly important, and left it to an incompetent apprentice to complete the job! I'm not doing this because I'm a lunatic, understand? I've spent two years with a psychiatrist to ensure that I'm mentally stable. I've got my clean chit for the operation. I *am* a bloody woman, deal with it!'

Antara nodded silently. She was taken aback by the tears glistening in Ajay's eyes. Despite the fact that they were unshed, they'd clotted his eyelashes, making them look spikier, thicker, longer and sexier – god, how she wanted him! She watched him get into the car and wave. She couldn't wave back. It was now that the full impact of his revelation hit her like a speeding truck and left her feeling achingly empty.

She locked herself in her bedroom and logged on to http://cruellycrushedlikeacockroach.blogspot.in for a long bout of self-pity. Her tear ducts were having such a wild party that, if she'd been pouring out her pain on paper, every single word would have been smudged.

To hell with this 'I'm a woman trapped in a man's body' shit, she thought miserably. Oh well, she gave Ajay credit for not using those clichéd words exactly, all he said was he'd decided to have a sex change. 'Unrequited love really stinks,' she muttered aloud.

All her life, the doggedly perseverant Antara had got what she wanted. If she wanted an essay to win first prize, she burned the midnight oil to ensure that it won. When she wanted a coveted job in a leading newspaper with a million better qualified people as contenders for the post, she went the extra mile to impress the interviewers. She had been sure she would succeed in dragging Ajay to the altar, screaming and kicking if need be. But this time, for the one and only thing that really mattered to her, something she'd have willingly bartered her soul to Mephistopheles for, she'd lost.

Antara scanned her memory bank for signs of Ajay's inner girl. It found many. He was a willing companion on her shopping sprees and he particularly enjoyed spending hours at the perfume counter with her, spraying testers on his wrists. Most incriminating was the fact that he absolutely refused to watch violent action movies like *Kill Bill* – that was proof that his testosterone levels were abysmally low. In fact, there was a strong possibility that Antara was more butch than Ajay had ever been.

Her memories also threw up clues that revealed that Ajay really did care about her. It reminded her of small, insignificant things like when they went to the movies with a crowd of friends, even if Ajay and she weren't seated next to each other, their eyes would instinctively seek each other out to acknowledge a witty piece of dialogue. Somehow, that made the joke funnier and more special. That was pure togetherness. Well. Couldn't they still be friends if they were the same sex, dammit?

Won't work, I lust him too much, she thought sadly and squeezed her eyes shut, hoping the action would shut him out of her mind too. Then suddenly, like a bolt out of the blue, a brilliant idea struck her: *Hello, if you want him that bad, you can bloody well become a lesbian!* Antara cheered up somewhat. All was not lost. She'd start by participating in LGBT parades. It would also be the perfect opportunity to wear the flamboyant magenta shirt with ruffles that she'd picked up on a crazy impulse at a flea market in Goa. It was buried under piles of relatively sober clothes in the wardrobe, waiting for its moment to shine. Antara delved into her cupboard and retrieved the ruffled shirt. Perfect! It just needed a spot of ironing.

As Ajay negotiated the traffic, he wished he were

going back to his bachelor digs instead of his parents' apartment. He idly wondered which of his parents he'd taken after. He'd got his delicate features from his mum, but that was about it. His brains were from his dad but that was about it too – he hadn't inherited the insane temper that could make raging bulls seem cuddly, or the ridiculously high testosterone levels either. And thank god for that! When he was younger, Ajay used to wonder if his distaste for his dad's temperament had subconsciously inspired him to stifle his male hormones. Well, either that, or the fact that he'd discovered he felt more at home in glittering green eye shadow when he'd played Desdemona at his all-boys' boarding school. He'd become hugely popular with his seniors after the play, and was frequently sought out for gropes in the dark. His parents were so caught up in their lives, they'd never discovered. Not even when his dorm master wrote them a letter euphemistically accusing Ajay of accepting sweets from boys. His mother had just sent him bigger parcels of chocolate and home-made fudge more often. Those days he'd fervently hoped he was just bisexual like a few of his school mates. But he was wrong, he'd discovered in his co-ed college years, when a tipsy Antara had dragged him into a bathroom during a party.

He parked the car outside his parents' building and got out reluctantly. A split second later he chickened out and shot back into the car, driving recklessly like a villain in a Bond movie car-chase sequence. He'd tell them after the surgery was over – only after. A fait accompli was what they deserved – besides, it would spare him his mum's tears, dad's threats and the emotional blackmail that would inevitably follow. It was his life anyway, goddammit.

He felt a lightness in his chest as he climbed the stairs to his paying-guest digs. Now *this* was home. A tiny matchbox built over a garage that shielded him from the prying eyes of the rest of the world. This was where he could be who he really was, a femme fatale in waiting, not a weedy apology for a man who couldn't protect his mother from an ogre.

He flung himself on the bed and lit a relaxing joint, reflecting on the new life that he would enter soon. Another sex. Another job. Another city. And another name. Not Ajaya, derived from Ajay. Something completely different and nondescript, the Indian equivalent of Jane Jones. There was only one tie he would maintain with the past: Antara. She was the only best friend Ajay had ever had, the only person he ever felt comfortable opening up to. A loner by nature, he had been bemused by her determined advances towards him at first. Antara had decided that she liked him the instant they had been introduced to each other, and had firmly taken him under her wing. He'd had no choice in the matter. Wherever he went, she was there too – not as a follower but as a partner. He'd been too polite to brush off her friendship gestures and a few weeks later was glad he hadn't – she was delightfully vivacious and absolutely adorable. It felt gratifying to be liked by her. And now, finally, he'd told her his biggest, deepest, darkest secret, and he felt so much better for having shared it with her. Despite the fact that she'd obviously been horrified at first and then utterly dismayed. She'd behaved like she'd been betrayed. Ajay, admittedly, was a wee bit indignant about her reaction. It wasn't *his* fault that she'd harboured a crush on him. It wasn't as though he'd callously led her on and then sprung an unpleasant surprise on her. He'd flashed innumerable signs that she had stubbornly chosen to ignore. The trouble with Antara was, if she wanted something, nothing in the world could make her stop wanting it. Just as well that she wasn't into illegal substances, Ajay grinned in the darkness – she'd probably be in jail by now, unreformed and unrepentant, determinedly bribing guards to get her dope.

Oh hell no! Ajay thought with a start and hurriedly dialled Antara's number.

'You will not, I repeat, not, pretend to become a lesbian so we can be a couple. Is that understood?' he said firmly.

'Don't be idiotic, Ajay,' Antara snapped. 'As if I'd even contemplate it!'

'Oh, okay. Sorry,' Ajay said apologetically.

After Antara disconnected the call, tears sprang to her eyes.

'See how well he knows me,' she wailed out loud to the four walls of her room that stared blankly back at her. 'I'll never ever find someone as wonderful as him again. We're perfect together!'

The magenta ruffled shirt was rolled into a ball and hurled into the cupboard rather violently.

Mexican hairless. That's what the boys at boarding school used to call Ajay. He'd even given up swimming to save himself from their constant jeers. It had started when they were in their early teens – they'd have competitions in the dorm, and the winner was the person with the most hair on his chest. But now, for perhaps the first time in his life, Ajay was glad that he wasn't a hairy ape. Hell, if he'd been like his father, he'd have had to rob a bank to pay for the electrolysis and laser treatment. The stubble had stopped showing by now. And the sessions with his gender therapist were almost over.

He'd done a few nights out in a wig and female attire too, as instructed by his surgeon, and the results had been flattering. He'd been whistled at and propositioned several times by roadside Romeos. One had even fondled his rear and been richly rewarded with a stinging slap. The most flattering part was that Ajay had just been in his regular baggy jeans and a pale blue tee when that eve-teasing incident had occurred. He hadn't switched to overtly feminine attire yet; he was saving that for after the surgery. A huge suitcase packed with satin lingerie, hip-hugging skirts and body-clinging tees. No lace or florals or baby pink for him, though. He wasn't going to be a wussy-fussy girl, no way. Just a chic chick.

The suitcase included a pack of sanitary napkins too. Antara had put those in to bring him down to earth. She'd viciously chosen extra large and lumpy post-natal napkins to exaggerate the horrors of menstruation. This was her desperate last-ditch attempt at persuading him to change his mind. Admittedly, this did put him off a bit, but his jovial surgeon reassured him that he would not menstruate or ever be able to have babies.

Ajay had chosen his doctor as carefully as he'd chosen his new clothes and accessories. He'd crossed three surgeons off the list soon after his furtive search began on the grounds of being too expensive, too cold and clinical and not experienced enough. Finally he found one who had just moved back to the country after years in the USA. The new surgeon was warm, reassuring and, better still, spoke his language. He was the sort of chap who would willingly hold his hand and guide him to a new life – a very crucial factor since Ajay did not have family support. The surgeon's sense of humour was the icing on the cake.

'I envy the man you marry,' the surgeon had told Ajay. 'No annoying coitus interruptus to find a condom and he won't have to tolerate the irritability that comes with pre-menstrual stress. I wish my neurotic wife had had a sex change before I married her too!'

Oh crap, he's married! Ajay thought with a momentary pang of disappointment. But even that cold, harsh fact didn't stop his heart from fluttering madly in the surgeon's presence. Drop dead sexy dude, that.

On the morning of Ajay's life-changing operation, the surgeon had a final piece of advice to offer:

'If I were you, I wouldn't casually go around telling people about the sex change. Family and exceptionally close friends are fine, but watch out for the others – there are a lot of nasty, judgmental people and perverts out there. The religious nuts who preach compassion are the nastiest of them all. If you spill the beans, there's a big chance that you won't get flowers, solitaires, chocolate and CDs by Justin Bieber. You will be wooed alright, but probably with raunchy Donna Summers's songs like 'Love to Love You Baby', throaty, exaggerated moans and whips and chains thrown in. Loads of deviant sex that you possibly may not enjoy.'

'Oh hell! Maybe I will tell the world about my sex change then – I hate, hate, hate Bieber!' was Ajay's spirited retort.

'Me too, I'm trying very hard to wean my daughter off him,' the surgeon grimaced. 'But honestly, do be discreet, okay? It's not as though people who are repulsed by sex change are evil – it's just that they have no imagination. If they stopped to think for a few moments what it may have been like if they had the same problem as you, perhaps they'd be more accepting.'

10, 9, 8, 7, 6, 5, 4, 3, 2, 1. The countdown had begun. As the anaesthesia began to make its deliciously slow and seductive sashay into Ajay's bloodstream, his mind lost its moorings and began to float like a long-suffering soul that had just been released from the body of an incredibly dull accountant. A flashback sequence of the highs and lows in his life paraded before him. Insights came to the fore as well, like the realization that grass was weedy shit compared to this mind-blowing stuff that was coursing through his veins. He needed more anaesthesia. Life had no meaning without it.

When he came to, the personal details on his curriculum vitae had changed along with his vital statistics. He was female, an orphan, brought up by grandparents long since dead. He'd studied at obscure schools and colleges in small-town India – the sort no city slicker could claim to know anybody from. He was just another vulnerable single girl looking for love.

Antara was there holding his hand and trying to stop herself from humming a song from Disney's *Cinderella* that was morbidly re-playing in her head: 'Bibbidi-Bobbidi-Boo'. She'd appropriately re-arranged it in her head as 'Bibbitty-Bobbitty-Boo'.

'How do I look?' Ajay whispered.

'The same,' she replied. 'Just sort of paler. How are you feeling?'

'Terribly sore and fuzzy, but happy.'

The surgeon entered and cheerily asked Ajay if

he'd like to keep his pound of flesh as a memento in a jar of formaldehyde.

'Bury or burn the damn thing!' Ajay howled. 'If we were living in a Greek tragedy, I could have fed it to my dad as moussaka.'

Antara felt her lunch rising. She rushed to the sink in the attached bathroom.

The surgeon laughed heartily and punched Ajay's arm, 'Now then, that's not a nice way for a delicate young lady to talk.'

Ajay grinned, beckoned the surgeon closer and whispered in his ear, 'Hey, can you get me some of this anaesthesia stuff?'

'No can do,' the surgeon replied, and then added with a broad wink, 'Study medicine. Every profession comes with its perks.'

After the surgeon left, Antara gave Ajay two presents: lacy lingerie and a book, *Goodbye Mr Chips*. She had an explanation for both.

'I've left the bill for the bra in the bag – they've agreed to exchange it for whatever size you want,' she said in a stilted voice. 'And as for the book, I didn't just choose this for you because the title is appropriate, which it *is*,' she added in a catty voice, 'but this is a small test to discover if the operation was truly successful.'

Ajay was bemused. He picked up the book and

speed-read the back-cover synopsis. 'Hello, how will a book about a doddering English schoolmaster throw light on the success of the operation?'

'You'll know if you feel a lump in your throat at the end of the book,' Antara said with her most supercilious look, almost like Owl in *Winnie the Pooh*. When she finally left, her goodbyes were accompanied by a vacant stare, not a warm, friendly smile. Not that Ajay noticed.

Ajay immersed himself in the book after she left. The lump in his throat speedily grew to the size of an adult elephant and then it dissolved into tears. He sobbed his way through the box of tissues on his bedside table. Oh yes, he definitely was a woman!

A horrifying thought struck him and he called Antara in a state of panic.

'Did you cry when you watched *Titanic*?'

'Well, almost, of utter boredom at its triteness. It was crap.'

'Whew, thank god. Because, Ant, if being a woman means that you cry at dumb movies like that, I want my pound of flesh back.'

Antara laughed dryly. 'I'll miss you when you go to Mumbai.'

'I'll miss you too. Wish I could persuade you to join me.'

'Oh well,' Antara sounded terse now, 'you've

decided to get on with your life, let me get on with mine too for heaven's sake, Ajay!'

'Anu.'

'Huh?'

'The name's Anu, not Ajay,' he said shyly. 'You like it?'

'Um, yes. Very nice. Bye.'

Antara could feel her voice quavering and hastily disconnected. With bitterness she realized that she was the one experiencing the worst side effects of Ajay's operation. She was the one who had gone through the bigger, more painful amputation.

After the phone call, Antara dragged herself out of bed and gave herself a critical once-over in the mirror. She wasn't beautiful, of that she was aware. She was too petite to be sexy. Neither was she voluptuous. Hell, Ajay would probably be better stacked than her in his new avatar. At best, she was cute. At worst, she was not *that* cute. However, in the right clothes, with the right make-up and the right tonal pitch, she could almost get there. She'd have a haircut first thing tomorrow. And buy seven push-up bras, one for each day of the week. Even if they didn't help achieve the physical miracles that the ads promised, they would, she hoped, uplift her sagging spirits.

She had to forget Ajay and reconstruct her life.

Meet other men who, fingers crossed, would stay that way. Out with the thigh-high skirts. On with the hunt for Ajay's successor. Right now, she'd take anything. Colour, caste, creed no bar. Only sex would be under microscopic scrutiny – and no metrosexuals sporting baby pink shirts, waxed chests and tweezed eyebrows would be tolerated either. My god, she'd been shockingly celibate for so many years, fervently hoping Ajay would give in to her. She'd played the devoted dog, yearning for him to say those magic words, 'Roll over', with a naughty gleam in his eyes. The command he'd finally given her was, 'Play dead'. Well, sort of. For her it was.

Soon after Ajay left for Mumbai, Antara started dating. Every week she went out with a different man though, oddly enough, they all had one thing in common: they were hard-core muscular gym jocks. In a moment of levity, Antara's father even referred to them in sequential order: Rambo 1, Rambo 2, Rambo 3 and so forth. And though Antara was working hard and partying harder, she still found time to write heart-wrenching daily posts at http://cruellycrushedlikeacockroach.blogspot.in.

Life wasn't exactly a bed of roses for Anu either.

After her metaphorical rebirth, she was a student at a catering college in Mumbai, and while she rather enjoyed her dramatically different profession, she wasn't too sure about anything else. She still hadn't told her parents. They'd never understand so what was the point, honestly? Time would tell her how to deal with this, she thought with a sigh. Just before her surgery, her parents had been given to believe that their son had been transferred to a small African nation with an unpronounceable name and an unreliable mail service because it was constantly at war ('internecine', Ajay had mumbled). That would do for now. It was far better to keep everything vague and hazy.

All Anu wanted was space, glorious space, to settle down comfortably in her new sex – that was right at the top of her ridiculously long 'To do' list. She also had another list titled 'Progress so far'. It read:

1. Voice therapy is working – my giggles have become charmingly girlie.
2. The potty seat at home is always down.
3. I own more cans of cockroach spray than baked beans.
4. I felt morbidly depressed, almost suicidal for weeks and weeks after I read Vikram Seth's *An Equal Music*. That's impressively girlie!

5. I have mastered the fake orgasm scene from Nora Ephron's fabulous film, *When Harry Met Sally*, yay! It isn't just Meg Ryan's parted lips, half-shut eyes and shuddering moans of ecstasy. Her hands play an important role too, fluttering down her arched neck, lingering at the base, and then suggestively tugging the neckline of her tee in an irresistibly slutty way.

There were negatives as well, but Anu had been too disheartened to list those down. Starting with the small embarrassing secret that she had merely perfected the *When Harry Met Sally* fake orgasm scene with the mirror as her indifferent glassy-eyed audience – she hadn't met anyone interesting yet. Oh, okay, she hadn't even been asked out yet! Perhaps because at five feet nine inches she was the tallest woman on campus and most of her male classmates looked up to her? Well, she fervently hoped it was just that.

Even more depressing, part of her had to concede that Antara had been right: being a woman was not all that terrific. Anu had to face the harsh fact that she had been brought up like a good, lazy Indian boy. Her mum had picked up after her, lovingly served food on her plate even after she was old enough to decide which political party should govern the country, ironed her underwear and treated her like an incarnation of God. She was used to being pampered. Now the mantle of play-up-to-the-male-ego-till-you-die-of-exhaustion had fallen on her frail shoulders. Men apart, getting a joint was like mission impossible. It was tough, as a woman, to hunt out weed.

It didn't help that although Anu had made a few let's-grab-a-coffee friends at the catering college, she was indescribably lonely. Antara had deserted her in her hour of need. She kept shrugging her off – Anu's frequent begging-for-companionship-oh-sharer-of-my-deep-dark-secret calls were answered alright, but Antara always had reasons to escape within three minutes. Her excuses were carelessly transparent: my favourite show is starting on TV/ got a killer of a deadline/eating dinner/out with friends, et cetera. She never did call back later. Anu was beginning to wonder if she was the one who had truly been betrayed – Ant wasn't acting supportive as best friends were meant to do, like that lovely R&B song went: 'Just call my name/I'll be there in a hurry/You don't have to worry/'Cause baby/There ain't no mountain high enough'. A part of her heart hardened over time and her calls to Antara became less frequent and finally petered out. Not that Ant noticed, Anu would sternly remind herself whenever she felt needy and desperate to hear Ant's voice.

Six months later, Anu fell in love, hallelujah. The man who made her bells not just ring but jangle violently like an urgent fire alarm was a publisher. After sampling her grilled Himalayan trout marinated in flaming bhut jolokia chilli at the catering college's amateur restaurant day, Rohit Sen barged into the dean's room to make Anu an offer only a fool would refuse: write a recipe book on modern Indian cuisine. The dean introduced Rohit to Anu, and after one look at her statuesque and deliciously androgynous body, Rohit impetuously added another proposition, 'Would you join me for dinner tonight? Please?'

Anu accepted. After all, she wasn't doing anything special that night, or any other night. The evening after, when Rohit sent her a bouquet of roses with a pretty parody of a Shakespearean sonnet ('Shall I compare thee to a 1995 Bordeaux red? Thou art more full-bodied and more heady.'), Anu was head over heels in love. She was so innocent she didn't ever bother to check on Google whether 1995 really was a good year for Bordeaux reds. Truth be told, she wasn't particularly fond of red wine either. What they say about love is true: it can turn Einsteins into idiots.

A few months later, Antara dumped her latest Rambo clone and decided he absolutely was her last sixteen-egg-whites-a-day gym jock. How long could she hang out with dimwits who thought *Free Willy* was a movie about a flasher? And who needed them any more, after she had finally worked out her unhappiness? As Antara's favourite writer Douglas Adams would have put it, she had passed through 'the long dark tea-time of the soul' and survived. She decisively deleted all her anguished posts on http://cruellycrushedlikeacockroach.blogspot.in one evening – she didn't need an outlet for her angst any more, much to the disappointment of the 17,866 followers of her blog worldwide. She was starting life on a clean page. If a weatherman had been consulted about her personality then, he'd have pursed his lips and said, 'Partly cloudy with occasional light showers'.

Now that Ajay was out of her system, Antara had room for Anu. So for the very first time after the sex-change surgery, Antara was the one to initiate a cozy chat. When Anu cheerfully answered the phone, Antara winced at her girlie tone, but just a little bit.

'Should I tear into you for ignoring me all these months or should I tell you about the love of my life?' Anu trilled.

'Er, suppose you start with the love of your life and gouge my eyes out later? Gossip always comes first!' Antara said with a sharp pang of guilt.

And so Anu gushed on and on and on about the incredible sexiness of Rohit Sen. Over an hour later, Antara had to invent an excuse to hang up because her phone ear felt like it was going to burst into flames. While she lay on her bed with an ice pack over her ear, she pondered over Rohit the Magnificent who smoked cigars, drank wine instead of water, ate truffles and foie gras for breakfast and wrote poems to Anu, mainly in French. Antara was not impressed. *How could Anu love a pretentious sod like that? Ajay would have laughed at him! Had the surgeon sneakily given him a sodding brain transplant as well?*

Updates on Rohit the Magnificent's romantic gestures and other annoying idiosyncrasies were duly given to Antara several times a week. It was just as well that the updates were relayed by phone or Anu may have been shocked by the expression of revulsion on Antara's face. Matters came to a head one morning, when Anu called with news.

Antara was in an edit meet. 'I'll call you back,' she said curtly, and Anu squealed, 'Cool, but hey, Ant, I just have to tell you this right now: I'm going to tell Rohit about my sex change tonight!' and then hung up.

Antara couldn't concentrate on the meeting and as soon as it was over she darted to an empty cabin and called Anu.

'Don't do it Anu, don't tell him now!' Antara barked into the phone.

Anu was a little taken aback at the urgency in Antara's voice.

'Well, I've got to tell him sometime, innit? And now's the best time, Ant. He's going to ask me to marry him tonight.' Anu felt effervescent little bubbles of euphoria bouncing and bursting inside her as she said that. She was qualified to write an essay entitled 'The Autobiography of a Bottle of Champagne'. The way she was feeling, she'd probably get seven out of ten for it – at the very least.

'And how do you know that?' Antara demanded.

Anu giggled. 'His personal assistant secretly told me. He sent her out to buy me a diamond ring! She's described it in vivid detail. I've got to tell him before he pops the question, right?'

Antara spluttered indignantly. 'What? What sort of person sends a personal assistant to buy an engagement ring?'

'A very busy person!' Anu sprang to Rohit's defence.

'He's just a bloody ass, Anu. Ajay wouldn't have stood for his crappy affectations,' Antara said, trying very hard not to lose her cool.

Anu, however, didn't bother to keep her temper in control. She performed a pretty decent imitation of a volcano erupting.

'Shut up! How dare you! And get out of my goddamn life, okay? You're always trying to put obstacles in my way so you can have me to yourself. Can't you get it into your thick head that I love you as a friend, just a friend? It's not my fault if you romanticized our friendship in your head, dammit! And what a lousy bloody friend you were. Where were you, my supposed best friend, when I needed you most after the surgery when I was alone and insecure? Go screw yourself!'

Anu disconnected, leaving a stunned Antara gasping to herself, 'Hey, I was only trying to help.' She was truly shocked. Ajay had never spoken to her like that. The only time he had ever raised his voice was when he had to hail a taxi. *Gosh, those female hormonal injections Anu's taking are fabulously potent*, she thought with deep respect. And then she brushed away a few salty tears of self-pity that had involuntarily trickled down her cheeks. Anu was wrong about her this time, dead wrong. She was being a best friend for a change, trying to warn Anu that it was too early in the relationship to reveal such a big secret – particularly not to a man who cared so deeply about what people thought of him. In Antara's books only the most insecure people in the world were name-dropping, brand-flaunting show-offs. Rohit the Magnificent wouldn't be able to deal with Anu's revelation, though Antara sincerely hoped she was wrong.

While Anu was deciding what to wear for her big night, Antara hurriedly threw a few things into a suitcase. She locked the suitcase and frowned – she was sure she'd forgotten something terribly important. A few seconds later, she rushed to the fridge, unlocked her suitcase and tossed a few jars of hazelnut chocolate spread into it.

Not for the first time in her life, Antara wished that they hadn't stopped the practice of serving alcohol on domestic flights. She was prepared to commit a political assassination for a drink or three. A few hours later, she rang Anu's doorbell anxiously. She tried a couple of times more and then dejectedly parked herself on the staircase and leaned her exhausted body against the grimy wall. She had nowhere else to go to in Mumbai and at 2 am she wasn't adventurous enough to start looking for a hotel. Just as well she had remembered to carry her cigarettes. Smoking gave her something to do.

A short while later, the ancient lift clattered upwards and Anu walked out alone. Antara silently observed her as she fumbled in her handbag for the door key. She was gorgeous, Antara admitted to herself – stunning model material with her long legs, slim hips and high cheekbones. Compared to Anu, she looked like cat's vomit.

After steeling herself, Antara stood up and cleared her throat.

'Hey,' she whispered.

Anu turned around with a start. Surprise turned to rage in an instant.

'You! Come to gloat, have you?' she said.

All Antara could hear, though, was the underlying hurt in her voice. So Rohit the Magnificent had turned into Rohit the Shit after all, damn.

'Look me in the eye and answer that question yourself,' Antara said as the door swung open.

Anu agitatedly ran her fingers through her hair. 'Look, I just need to be alone, okay?'

'And I need a place to stay – for just one night?

I'll take the sofa, you lock yourself in the bedroom if you want,' Antara said gently.

'This is goddamn Mumbai – it's a one-room apartment, dammit!' Anu screamed and burst into tears.

Several tablespoons of hazelnut chocolate spread later, Antara found out that after Rohit's initial shock-and-horror moment at Anu's confession, he had been more excited than dismayed. The sparkly diamond ring that Anu knew for sure was in his jacket pocket hadn't been offered, though. She could even see the bulge of the box. Or perhaps she'd imagined she could see it because his personal assistant had told her it was there?

'He wants us to go shopping for sex toys tomorrow,' Anu whispered.

'And you agreed?' Antara shrieked.

Anu shrugged indifferently.

'What choice do I have? Every man I meet will probably suggest the same when he finds out.'

'No, they won't!' Antara thundered.

'Yes, they will. The surgeon had warned me, but I foolishly hoped he was wrong,' Anu said and her face crumpled. 'I made a mistake, Ant, the sex change was a big mistake. I'm a bigger freak than I was before. I should have kept the girl in me trapped in my body. I could have lived without love. But to live in a state of humiliation for the rest of my life – I just don't know how to deal with it,' she wailed.

Antara wrapped her arms around Anu. 'You're not going back to being Ajay, okay?' she said fiercely. 'You were meant to be a girl and you're the loveliest girl ever. Don't let one bastard get you down. Now, pay attention – you're never seeing Rohit again, understood?'

Anu's silence made Antara want to scream. A glint of steely determination flashed in her eyes. She swore to herself that she'd find a decent man for Anu. A man who had enough self-confidence to take anything on. Someone who could perhaps afford to bathe in champagne but was secure enough to drink an inexpensive brand of rum in public because he enjoyed the taste. A man who didn't give a damn about what people thought of his personal choices. Antara was determined to work extra hard on a list of attributes for an ideal man. She wouldn't rest till she found one for Anu. And one for herself too, while she was about it.

'Do you have a laptop handy?' Antara scanned the room impatiently.

Anu eyed her warily. 'Not if you're putting my name on a matrimonial site,' she said.

'Nope. Just writing to my editor for an instant transfer to Mumbai. He owes me big time for covering for him when he goofed up on the facts in a high-profile political piece. I took the rap for it. Almost lost my job, in fact. '

Anu's mascara-streaked eyes widened. 'You're doing this for me? When I was so nasty to you?'

'Big deal, you didn't know better. After all, you used to be a man. And men, as we all know, are damn fools,' Antara said magnanimously.

Anu dug her spoon into the half-empty jar of hazelnut chocolate spread and scooped up a large helping. 'Amen to that,' she said with a faint smile. A little later, the faint smile widened to a broad grin and Anu found herself screaming with laughter as Antara related anecdotes of her dates with the Rambo series of men. She was at her bitchiest best.

Anu learnt her first valuable girlie lessons that night – more valuable than the fake orgasm scene she'd mastered from *When Harry Met Sally*.

1. Every girl absolutely must have a 3 am friend.
2. Every girl must keep a jar of hazelnut chocolate spread in the fridge for emergencies. For while hazelnut chocolate spread cannot mend broken hearts, it does a fabulous job of easing the pain.

4

Heavy Weather

I first bumped into Sid at an airport waiting lounge. He looked very familiar and I stared at him shamelessly, trying to place him. He definitely wasn't a Bollywood star, of that I was certain. I mean, he wasn't wearing rouge or nude lipstick, and his brow looked furrowed, not telltale Botox-smooth. He looked amused as he caught my stare and I hastily looked away, embarrassed, burying my burning face in my newspaper.

A husky voice on the PA system announced that my flight was delayed indefinitely because of heavy rain – which meant that the breakfast I'd anticipated while airborne was delayed. Really annoying because I had only eaten a small piece of tandoori chicken the night before, inspired by an article that sternly said words to the effect of, 'Do not eat carbs at night or else you'll turn into a gigantic pumpkin that's worthy of winning a gold medal at a local agricultural show'. I drifted towards the snacks counter and stared morosely at the selection of stale, uninspiring sandwiches. My nose wrinkled involuntarily. The green stuff in most of them looked more like fungus than cilantro chutney.

'How many years old are these sandwiches?' I sniffily asked the man at the counter.

He scowled at me fiercely, but the person standing next to me guffawed.

'Now now, that's not a very nice thing to say – I'm sure those sandwiches are not more than a few months old.'

I wheeled around to face him – it was the same man I'd been caught staring at! I blushed deeply and launched into a fervent apology.

'Hey, you know, I wasn't staring at you because I think you're hot. I mean, it's not that you're not hot, but it's just that your face looks very familiar,' I stuttered. 'Maybe we worked somewhere together before?'

'Only if you've worked for a news channel,' he said with a faint smile.

The penny dropped.

'Oh right, you're that guy I saw on TV last night standing in eight-inch deep water with an umbrella over your head and a mike in your hand, looking like a drowned rat,' I exclaimed.

He grimaced. 'Yeah, I'm that drowned rat.

Actually, right now, I'm more like a dead rat. Got a very bad cold. I'm Siddharth– *a-ti-shoo*!' He sneezed as he held out his right hand.

I clasped it and said, 'Nice to meet you, Siddharth A-ti-shoo. I'm Anya Singh.'

He laughed and I didn't demur when he offered to take me to the exclusive executive lounge for breakfast – open only to business-class travellers. He warmly assured me that the sandwiches there weren't more than a few hours old.

It was lovely – the company, not the sandwiches! Sid was vastly entertaining – he had a repertoire of anecdotes, mainly about politicians. Those men in khadi kurtas really live it up. Some of them can make Hugh Hefner look angelic. Time flew, and we had lunch there too. Oddly enough, I didn't scream and shout or kick furniture like I usually do when the voice on the PA system announced that all flights in and out of Mumbai were cancelled for the day. I was perfectly willing to have dinner at the executive lounge and breakfast there the next day as well, as long as Sid was around. He was dead sexy.

Sid had other plans, though. He was feeling feverish, and decided that we should check into the nearest hotel as soon as possible before the rooms were taken – there was bound to be a rush with the flights cancelled, he said. What a waste of money booking two rooms was, considering that we eventually spent the night in just one. Not being naughty, though – I was merely playing Florence Nightingale to the poor, sniffling chap! I tucked him into bed and leaned back on a comfy armchair but before the night was out, we were snuggled up together under the duvet, chatting about life, the universe and everything. Midway through, Sid croaked that he was in love with me already. I was certain he was delirious – and I was pretty sure that I was deliriously in love!

Sid was still sleeping when the room-service chap arrived with the breakfast I'd ordered. I wanted to give him a tip, but since I had nothing lower than 500-rupee notes in my bag, I searched Sid's wallet for change. A photograph of a little boy who looked just like him fell out! My heart sank. Oh, so the jerk was married, was he? I was hugely pissed off.

I swiftly cleared out of his room while he was still sleeping. Believe me, I want nothing to do with married men. There are lots of things I wish I could be in life: a lead guitarist in a rock band, a song writer, sometimes even an artist – being a mistress, however, has never been one of my childhood aspirations. Hey, I like to own my men!

I checked out of the hotel and made for the airport. The rain was letting up and we were assured that flights would take off soon. I moodily mooched around the airport lounge, half of me wishing that I wouldn't spot Sid, the other half fervently hoping that I would. Chances were, we wouldn't meet because he was taking a flight to Patna to report on floods in Bihar, and I was going home to Delhi. Damn! Life just wasn't fair.

I almost missed my flight. I had fallen asleep in my hard plastic chair before the boarding announcement was made, and I thought I was dreaming when I heard my name being called repeatedly. I leapt up and rushed to the gate waving my boarding card, when I heard my name being called again – not on the PA system this time.

My heart lurched. Sid's hair was tousled, his eyes were fiery red and he looked like he'd gone through agony to find me – sort of like how I imagine Brontë's Heathcliff. And then I remembered that he had a son. And a raging fever too – that explained his wretched appearance. I sharply turned on my heel and marched outside the gate when he called out to me again.

'Why did you leave without saying goodbye?' he hollered.

I didn't want to announce to the airport that I'd spent the night with a married man, so I cryptically (and coldly) said, 'Your son looks just like you.'

'What son?' he shouted, looking puzzled.

'What do you mean "what son"? How many do you have?' I shouted back with a glare. It's difficult being cryptic when you have only a few seconds to frame your sentences.

'I didn't say which son, I said, *what* son? What's with your grammar? And I don't have a goddamn son! Or a daughter either! Not even a dog,' he added unnecessarily.

'I saw a photograph of a little boy in your wallet!' I screamed. And I really had to scream because a plane was taking off.

'That's my nephew, you moron!'

I experienced this irrepressible urge to fling myself into his arms, and I would have done it if the impatient airport staff hadn't shoved me into the waiting bus. As the bus jerked to a start and sped towards the aircraft, I blew kisses at him. He continued to scowl at me like the man at the sandwich counter.

Despite the fact that I was sneezing furiously and felt mildly feverish on the flight back home, I had a silly smile on my face. I had it completely worked out: we lived in the same city, we had each other's phone numbers. We'd pick up from where we'd left off, of that I was certain. I saw him on TV that night somewhere in Bihar. His umbrella was aloft and the water knee-deep. He sneezed rather a lot. I couldn't stop giggling even though my heart went out to him.

Sid never called me, though. I waited like a lovesick teenager by the phone, willing it to ring, but it never did. And whenever I tried calling him, his phone was switched off. Even more dispiriting was the fact that I never saw him on TV again – and god, I watched every single weather capsule on every single news channel daily! I'm not the sort to give up easily, particularly not when I meet someone that sexy who can also make me laugh. Fortunately, I knew the name of his TV channel. I called his office everyday for over a week. Each time, I was told that he wasn't in. I eventually stopped calling when the operator sympathetically informed me that Sid didn't work there any more. I called every other news channel in the country thereafter. Nope. Not there. He had vanished into thin air.

I'm sorry to report that several trees were murdered over a man I met for just one day in my life – I sobbed through many boxes of tissues and often wondered whether I should substitute my pillow with a giant sponge. It was only after the monsoon finally retreated that I forlornly decided to move on.

Months later, on a foggy winter's night, I spotted Sid at a restaurant – I was dining there with a man who had boyfriend potential. But one look at Sid and I knew that I still wanted him as badly as I had before. I was perfectly willing and able to yank him by the hair, toss him over my shoulder and take him home.

Once again, Sid caught me staring shamelessly at him. This time I didn't blush or avert my eyes hastily. I looked meaningfully at him instead and raised my eyebrows. He seemed delighted to see me – I got a sunny smile in response. Of course, I was hugely relieved to note that he was just with a bunch of guys. If he'd been accompanied by a woman, I may not have done what I did. Unless, of course, she looked old enough to be his mother.

I excused myself from the table on the pretext of powdering my nose – I wanted to see if Sid would follow. I parked myself on a sofa outside the restroom and my heart hammered so violently against my ribcage I was afraid it would crack open. I exhaled when Sid arrived with a dead sexy smile plastered on his face. It took all the strength I had to suppress the urge to hurl myself into his arms.

Far be it from me to waste time on niceties like, 'Hello, how are you, does your dog still have ticks?'

'Why didn't you call?' I snapped at him.

'Hey, I didn't have your number. My phone got washed away in the Bihar floods.'

'You could have browsed through the city telephone directory! Or was it too heavy for you to lift?' I sneered.

Sid sighed. 'Oh come on, Anya, I had no clue how to find you – you merely said that you were a graphic designer, you never bothered to tell me where you worked. You're not on Google either! And, incidentally, I did lift the heavy city telephone directory frequently – I'm not a ninety-eight-pound weakling who gets sand kicked in his face by bullies at the beach! Biceps don't lie,' he demonstrated, flexing his muscles.

They were, I noted approvingly, in super shape.

'Trust me, I called over two zillion Singhs listed in the phone book. It was madness! I cursed your family for not having an unusual surname like Mathurkar or Subujee or Chattermanium or Patkarani or something that stood out.'

I had to concede that Sid had a point. In Delhi practically every other person is a Singh. He'd won that round hands down.

We sat side by side on the sofa, catching up. My life had been dull and boring compared to his. The poor chap had been languishing in hospital for three months after the Bihar weather-report assignment, with a deathly combination of pneumonia and leptospirosis. Covering the weather appears to be more dangerous than covering wars! When he eventually recovered, his parents absolutely insisted that he quit the television industry and join the family business.

'And what business would that be?' I asked. I seriously hoped he wouldn't be in starchy finance.

'Manufacturing shower heads,' he said with a huge grin.

'Gosh, you can't seem to escape showers! Karmic, huh? I hope you turn the geyser on before you test them in future,' I giggled. But I was really concerned about his health. I was crazy about this man!

His lips twitched. 'Yeah, but I'd rather turn something else on instead. Or, rather, *someone* else.'

Then his eyes darkened suddenly. 'So,' he asked me archly, 'who *is* that guy who was looking deep into your eyes?'

'Just some random person,' I shrugged, smiling innocently at him.

'Hmm. Are you going to break his heart?' He looked at me searchingly as he said that.

'Let's see, that depends,' I pondered deeply.

'On what?' he prodded, nudging me. Oh, it was wonderful feeling his warmth after ages. I was so looking forward to testing shower heads with him. Truckloads of them. I hoped his family manufactured jacuzzis as well. I would bring my own bubble bath!

'Well, only if you don't lose my number again!' I said, looking as stern as it's possible to look when your heart is doing crazy cartwheels.

I fished out my business card from my bag, scribbled my cell phone number on it too and handed it to Sid with a flourish. Then I reluctantly walked back to my candle-lit table. Heck, I'd spent about half an hour away from my date – he'd probably assumed I had diarrhoea or some other non-sexy ailment.

I'd just about reached the table when my phone began to ring. I said a brisk 'hello' and then whispered to my date, 'Sorry, I have to take this call – it's my sister.'

He nodded indulgently and patted my hand.

I frowned deeply first while I listened, and then squealed into the phone.

'What? You've got chickenpox? Oh crap! That means Mum, Dad and I are in trouble too!'

I disconnected the call and looked up to see my date squirming in his chair.

'You haven't had chickenpox before, I gather,' I said dryly.

He shook his head violently and, even though I'm not a mind reader, I could clearly tell that he was kicking himself for patting my hand earlier on.

'Oh well, you and I could spend quarantine together, I guess. Quality time and all that,' I smiled coquettishly.

I was left alone to pay the bill – but not for long.

Sid joined me a few seconds later.

'You'll have to say you're HIV+ when you want to dump me, but let me warn you now, young lady, even that won't work,' he grinned.

'Not even if I really am HIV+?' I asked.

He reached for my hand.

'Nope – medical science has made great advances. Hey, don't you read the papers?'

The Friendship Diaries

1

The Ex-Files

7 days to Christmas

I knew it! I knew it! I knew it! The second the gorgeous new girl sashayed into the conference room, I just knew it was only a matter of time before Arjun would give me that tired old 'It's not you, it's me' cliché. What makes men think that we'll hate them less for dumping us if they solemnly confess that they're valuable case-study material for shrinks? When I saw the way Arjun looked at Pervin as the introductions were made, I sent an instant message to God in my head: *Make sure Pervin's happily married or I won't attend midnight mass to celebrate your son's birthday.* I meant it.

Pervin was single, rats. So it happened sooner than I thought it would – it took Arjun less than a week to dump me at the coffee shop next to office. 'We need to talk,' he said with a hangdog expression on his face. I knew what was coming, and I decided to make it harder for him. I reached for his hand and squeezed it tight. 'Yippee, finally! Yes, I *will* marry you, cuddle bunny,' I said with fake exuberance. I wish I'd been quick enough on the uptake to click a photograph on my cell phone of Arjun squirming with embarrassment. He hurriedly stuttered and stammered the 'It's not you, it's me' line before I could start blabbering about what we'd name our children. I was determined not to feed his male ego by crying as he ham-handedly let me down – heck, I'd been expecting it anyway. Instead, I kept myself strong and poker-faced by mentally swearing to myself that the next time a guy tells me 'It's not you, it's me', I will kick him where it hurts – and I don't care if he won't be able to have babies thereafter.

Mum and Dad weren't home when I got back, which was a relief. My bravado vanished into thin air when I entered my bedroom and saw the outfit I had neatly laid out on my chair for the party Arjun and I had been expected to attend tonight. I wondered if Pervin would accompany him there or he'd take her to an intimate dinner instead – that was more his style. I flung myself face down on the bed and had a good cry till I heard the door-handle squeak as it was turned. *Note to self: Must remember to get the bedroom latch fixed to keep Mum from sneaking in.*

'Goodness, you're home early,' Mum said. One look at my face and she muttered, 'Uh oh, you didn't go to that party, then.' Normally, I don't tell Mum anything. I don't like to encourage conversation with her because frankly she irritates me by trying to play my best friend. It's bad enough that she borrows my strappy tees without asking, pinches my CDs for her car and witters on about how so and so saw us at the Catholic Gymkhana and thought we were twins. And when Arjun comes over, well, when he used to come over, she'd join us in the living room and monopolize the conversation. It would be one thing if she merely groaned about lumbago and things people her age suffer from, but no – she'd act as though she were *our* age, and moan about some rock star's thighs. Oh, come on! She'd even sent Arjun a friendship request on Facebook – he had no choice but to accept it. As for me, I blocked her!

Tonight, though, I was distraught enough to tell her and I didn't flinch like I usually do when she babies me with hugs and cuddles. After my sobs turned to less frequent sniffs, I told Mum that I was going to resign first thing on Monday.

'Absolutely not,' Mum said firmly. 'You love your job and you're not going to let a stupid man get in the way of your career.'

She didn't relent, not even when I told her about

Arjun making a play for Pervin and how awkward it would be for me to work in the same office.

'Did Arjun bring up that "We can still be friends" rubbish?' Mum asked. She was gazing into the distance with a faint smile playing on her lips. Actually, it was more of a smirk than a smile.

I nodded and informed Mum that when I told him I'd rather be hit by a garbage truck, he'd looked relieved. Hugely relieved.

'You're such a silly, impetuous girl,' Mum said fondly and ruffled my hair. I shrank away from her touch. Hello, she was supposed to be comforting me, not pointing out my character flaws.

'Now listen to me, and listen good,' Mum said. 'When I was your age, a man broke up with me and asked if we could be friends. I accepted because I wanted him any which way, and soon after we got married and had you. '

'*Dad* gave you that crap?' I squeaked. I was so astonished I forgot about my pain for a second.

Mum's eyes twinkled. 'Men are not very bright – you just have to learn to play them wisely.'

So now I'm deciding whether to go with my gut and quit my job, or go out on a limb and get Arjun back. I want him. I need him. I cannot imagine life without that slimy creep.

6 days to Christmas

I called a carpenter first thing in the morning and got my bedroom latch fixed. I need my privacy like never before – aunties, uncles and cousins keep popping in with homemade cakes, marzipan squares and kulkuls. I hate it when they inquisitively ask, 'Where's that nice Hindu boy you're dating?' Mum was marvellous. The first time someone brought Arjun up, she said he's not partying this year because someone died. We have stuck to that story. Even Dad doesn't know that the someone who died is me.

I'm getting angrier by the second: Arjun shouldn't have dumped me just yet. Couldn't he have waited till after Christmas? The slimeball knows how important it is to me!

On second thought, I'm willing to concede that maybe Arjun did do me a favour by dumping me during my party season. All my relatives are too drunk on Jesus's blood to notice that I disappear to the bathroom frequently and my eyes are red when I emerge. I still hate him, though.

5 days to Christmas

I want to move into a hotel! After the church service, the house was crawling with relatives and I had no space to cry. Not even my bathroom was free – all that wine and cake had made the diabetic aunties and uncles queue up for the loos. Mum noticed my distress and whispered, 'Go to a friend's place. I'll tell the horrors here that you haven't done your Christmas shopping yet. Go on, scram! I'll make sure the house is guest-free by 6 pm.' The aunties gasped when Mum told them her big fat lie. I was reprimanded for being so tardy and old Auntie Bernie hollered that she wants pretty knickers as a present but not nylon ones with frothy lace – they make her feel itchy.

I was so grateful to Mum for getting me out of the Sunday family lunch that I didn't shout at her for pinching my red halter-neck tee. Why does she insist on wearing clothes that don't suit her? And couldn't she ask me if she could borrow it, at the very least?

I didn't go to a friend's place because I didn't feel like talking about Arjun – not yet. I actually did go to a mall to finish my Christmas shopping. I bought Mum a sophisticated scarf – it's the palest of pale lilacs. It's about time she dressed with dignity. I must say that this mall has very nice loos where you can cry peacefully for hours. You just have to be shameless enough to ignore the glares when you emerge.

Mum and Dad put up the Christmas tree in the evening. I noted that the tree was the perfect size to shove up Arjun's ass and a smile crept onto my face as I pictured it. Mum caught me smiling and smiled back like she could read my mind. Then she winked at me. Good god, I'm beginning to wonder if we're alike!

4 days to Christmas

I get Monday-morning blues every Monday, but today was the worst ever. I crept into office with my resignation letter typed and ready to hand over. I had planned to tell my boss that I wouldn't be serving my notice period so feel free to deduct money from my salary blah blah. Arjun entered my cabin while I was slumped over my desk waiting for my boss to arrive. He said hello with a tender smile and solicitously asked me how I was doing, as though I had a terminal disease. Something in me snapped.

'Hey, bestie!' I jumped up and high-fived him.

He looked gobsmacked as I rattled on about how I had changed my mind about being friends. He gave me a fake smile, put on his busy face and strode away.

His fleeting expression of fear mingled with astonishment made me tear my resignation letter into tiny shreds. I was on to something!

Admittedly, I did take two tiny breaks in the day to weep in the loo. The first time was during lunch break when Arjun parked himself on Pervin's desk and she giggled up at him. The second was when I overheard him calling her 'cupcake' while we were in a meeting in the conference room: 'Pass me the slides, cupcake,' he'd whispered. He'd never referred to me as a dessert item ever, and it really bothered me. Why hadn't he called me blueberry cheesecake/ tiramisu/chocolate mousse before? Evidently he liked her more than he had liked me and that hurt. I wasn't even muffin enough for him!

Mum called later in the afternoon to check on me. 'I assume you haven't quit since you're not home yet. Congratulations!' she said in a hearty voice.

'Oh Mum,' I sighed and told her all. She laughed uproariously at the 'Hey, bestie' bit and clucked over the dessert reference. She urged me not to give up. 'Go hang out where he's hanging out, chat with them, become friends with Pervin and always remember to slap him on the back, ruffle his hair and things like that in front of her. And keep calling him "bestie", okay?'

I followed Mum's instructions and they worked like a charm. Every free moment I had the rest of that day was spent with Pervin – I stuck it out even though she didn't look particularly welcoming. Arjun stayed away as long as he could but finally he couldn't take being separated from his loved one any more. Besides, I bet he was dying to know what I was up to.

'Hey, bestie,' I gurgled as he came up. 'Pervin says you guys are seeing a movie tonight. I'd love to come.'

Arjun turned pale. 'Tell you what,' I continued, 'it's on me as a Christmas present to you guys. And dinner after is my treat as well, okay?' I pinched Arjun's cheek as I said that. He could hardly have refused.

I sent a text message to Mum and she responded with, 'YOU GO GIRL!' Yes, all caps. Who does she think she is, Oprah? The movie was a tear-jerker, but I couldn't stop smiling to myself in the dark. Dinner was even more fun. Arjun and Pervin barely exchanged a word since I dominated the conversation with riveting anecdotes about the days when Arjun and I had first met two years ago.

'Oops, I had no idea Arjun and you used to date,' Pervin said, looking embarrassed and a wee bit uncomfortable. The poor thing was just a few days old at the office, she couldn't have known Arjun's dating history. Besides, company policy frowns on relationships at the workplace, so Arjun and I had kept ours under wraps.

I waved my hand dismissively. 'Oh, that was a long, long time ago, right Arjun?'

Arjun stared at his lamb chops. I let it go.

By the end of the evening – and I made it drag till past midnight – I knew Pervin was slightly wary of me. As for Arjun, I'm sure he's beginning to hate me – not as much as I hate him, though. I'm still working on it! The icing on the cake was, I insisted on dropping Pervin home in a cab. She did make a feeble attempt to get out of it, but I insisted. 'Hey, it's no problem – you're on my way. And my bestie's looking so exhausted I just have to pitch in,' I said affectionately and ruffled Arjun's hair.

Mum was waiting up for me and we fell into each other's arms and laughed till we cried.

I spent over three grand tonight but it was so worth it!

3 days to Christmas

Mum's a thoughtful person. Every year she bakes an extra Christmas cake for my team of fourteen colleagues at the office, cuts it into generous slices and wraps them individually in cling film so they don't get messy. I always hand them out on the evening of the office Christmas party. This year, it was no different. Well, there was a small difference. When Mum gave me the plastic container with the cake, she warned me that there was a slice with a tiny dot of red nail polish on the wrapper. She picked out the slice and waved it under my nose. 'This is especially for Arjun. Make sure no one else gets it, will you?'

I panicked. Annoying Arjun was one thing, poisoning him was not permissible, however.

'Don't be silly – I wouldn't dream of poisoning any living creature, not even a rat. I've just added a dash of something your granny takes when she has to go,' Mum said reasonably.

'Go where?' I asked, puzzled.

'To the bathroom.'

'No way,' I told Mum sternly.

'Suit yourself,' she shrugged and warned me that I may not have such a wonderful time at the office party when they started playing slow music and

Arjun and Pervin melted into each other's arms. I got the point. I had to be sure first, though.

'Are you absolutely, positively certain it won't kill him? Have you tried this before?' I asked Mum.

She nodded impatiently.

'Your granny's still alive, isn't she?'

At 6 pm I handed out the cake to everyone but Arjun. He got special treatment – I lovingly shoved his slice into his mouth while Pervin was watching. 'For you, bestie!' I cheerfully said, and carefully wiped the crumbs off his face with a wet tissue which I later flushed down the potty – it's important not to leave evidence lying around.

The party began at a neighbouring hotel at 7 pm. Arjun's fireworks still hadn't begun. I began to worry that Mum hadn't added enough of Granny's 'to go' herbs. At 8.15 pm, Arjun was missing in action. He returned half an hour later and kept disappearing for long stretches. I hung around with Pervin to make sure she wasn't lonely, and out of the kindness of my heart introduced her to the super stud from the investment banking division who I happened to know was single.

Arjun left before 10 pm. And at 11 pm, when the music slowed down to schmaltz, I felt a warmth steal into my heart as I watched Pervin and the super stud from the investment banking division dance without an inch between them. I left the party soon after. Mission accomplished.

When I got home, I told Mum this was the best Christmas present she'd given me ever.

2 days to Christmas

Pervin didn't smile at me when she arrived at the office late the next morning – she beamed like a sun goddess and parked a gigantic slab of chocolate on my desk.

'Oooh thanks, what's this for?' I asked, innocence oozing out of every pore.

'Christmas, of course!' she said with a grin.

Arjun slunk into office much later, looking weak and pale. He didn't smile at me either – he glared and confronted me.

'What did you put in that cake?' he said. I didn't approve of his body language – there was more than a hint of menace in his posture.

'Huh? Is there a problem?' I meekly said.

Arjun repeated his question. I didn't answer it directly. I stepped into the corridor, raised my voice and asked everyone in my team if they had had the runs after eating Mum's cake.

The answer was no. Pervin's voice was the loudest, I was happy to note.

I dramatically whipped out my cell phone and punched Mum's number on the keypad. 'Hey, I didn't bake the cake, my mum did. Why don't you tell her that she tried to poison you yourself, okay Arjun?' I said angrily.

Mum answered and I urgently said, 'Mum, someone here has a complaint about your cake.' I tried to hand the phone to Arjun but he backed away. He got withering looks from everyone as he slunk down the corridor.

Pervin snatched the phone out of my hand and spoke to Mum warmly. 'She's just kidding. The cake was lovely, thank you very much. Hang on a minute, please,' she said and addressed our teammates.

'Hey, let's thank Mrs Correa on speakerphone, guys!'

Cheers and applause for Mum rang out in the corridor.

Just when I thought that nothing could get better, the super stud from investment banking joined Pervin at her cubicle for lunch. They really look good together. Both of them are gorgeous.

I spent the rest of the day at work humming, ''Tis the season to be jolly'.

Late at night, I sent Mum a friendship request on Facebook.

Christmas Eve

I left office after lunch today – I had something very important to do. I went to the mall and exchanged the sober pale lilac scarf I'd got for Mum for an electric purple strappy tee. After all these years, I'd finally discovered what suited her best. After the shop girl gift-wrapped it, I scribbled 'Merry X'mas, bestie' on the card. It wasn't just a private joke between Mum and me – I meant it.

Christmas Day

I did go to midnight mass eventually last night. Mum insisted that it would be nice to thank God for teaching me forgiveness. 'After all, you still stayed friends with Arjun even though he let you down so badly,' she said.

'Oh, absolutely,' I agreed.

2

Best Friends and Boyfriends

Tuesday

11 pm: Damn! Double damn! Triple damn! Ambika's still not answering the phone and there will be icky sticky bits of me splattered all over the bedroom walls if I don't get to speak to her right this minute! I'm ready to explode with rage. She has absolutely no business to treat Ravi in that shabby manner. I hate the way she looks at him with her nose wrinkled distastefully as if he's a smelly crow-pecked rat with its entrails exposed. And I can't stand the glazed look in her eyes when he directs remarks at her. WTF! She's been my best friend since kindergarten – she's honour-bound to make an attempt to be civil to my boyfriend. And if that's not a law, I'm going to campaign madly across the nation to make it one – severe punishment will follow if you treat your best friend's boyfriend with undisguised contempt, like three bleak years without access to the Internet. Not even Google or Wiki for vitally important research purposes. So there!

11.27 pm: The bitch is *still* not answering the phone. I bet she's doing this on purpose because she knows how badly she behaved at dinner tonight. Uh oh, my phone's ringing. It had better be that s*%$!

11.45 pm: I really let her have it, no holds barred. She slimily tried to wriggle out of it by saying that I had treated her recent ex like garbage, so what was the big deal. Yeah well, I sneered, the big deal was I *knew* he was garbage – he was beating her black and blue and I wasn't falling for her 'I walked into a door, I tumbled down the stairs, I slipped on the bathroom floor' excuses any more. Honestly, why she put up with him for so long beats me. He wasn't even nice-looking and his IQ would be just about average. 'Yes, but Anurag had a great sense of humour,' Ambika said weakly in his defence. I shortly told her that if beating women was so funny stand-up comics would be including it regularly in their acts, wouldn't they? She abruptly disconnected the call and I am still seething with rage. She hedged without answering my most important question: why was she so nasty to Ravi when she was meeting him for the first time? She knew nothing, absolutely nothing about him so she could have made an attempt to be pleasant, at least!

11.55 pm: Tried calling her again but her phone is switched off! Have sent her a nasty private message on Facebook. And if she doesn't respond by tomorrow morning – okay, I'll give her till 6 pm since we go back to the good old days when we tunelessly sang the alphabet song together in school – I will ruthlessly unfriend her!

Wednesday

6.05 pm: Have unfriended Ambika – may she get wrinkles before she turns thirty! P.S. And may she be visibly allergic to Botox.

7.30 pm: Met Ravi at the lounge bar. Was in the mood for comforting snacks like crumb-fried mozzarella sticks and bruschetta, but he brusquely vetoed the idea. He ordered Thai raw papaya salad and, yup, that's it! 'Erm, if we're having salad then could it be Caesar salad with chicken?' I suggested hopefully. Ravi shook his head and my heart sank like the Titanic. I must have looked as glum as I felt because Ravi earnestly explained that his boss had circulated an e-mail extolling the joys of being vegan this morning so he had decided to check it out. 'He's so damn fit for his age, I want to be just like him,' he said enthusiastically. I felt less than enthusiastic about his decision – hey, nothing makes me happier than steak and bacon – but I nodded dumbly. My mood lifted a second later when Ravi reached out for my hand and squeezed it gently, saying, 'You will be supportive of my decisions, won't you?' Gosh, I felt bolts of electricity crackling through my body at his touch. Right then my hormones danced like dervishes and I would have cheered madly at almost anything he suggested – except supporting nasty right-wing parties, of course. Lines must be drawn. I smiled lovingly at him and squeezed his hand back.

Nonetheless, I whined for garlic bread at the very least, and he relented with an indulgent smile – he told the waiter that it must be multigrain or whole wheat and absolutely no butter. On the upside, we drank a lot of expensive wine and a good time was had by all. The only blot on the landscape was when my phone rang on the drive back home. I glanced at it and swiftly cut the call when I saw it was from Ambika. But she never gave up – she called yet again despite my pointed call-cutting-off rebuff. My god, she was behaving like I was a lover who had unfriended her on Facebook. Ridiculous! I switched the phone off, cursing her in my head.

'Why don't you get that? It could be important,' Ravi asked, looking at me with surprise. I shook my head mutinously. 'It's only Ambika. And I hate, hate, hate her,' I said sulkily.

'Hey, any enemy of yours is an enemy of mine,' he said robustly and we both giggled. And then he said that last night he'd been wondering what Ambika and I had in common. He pointed out her manhole-sized bindi with a visible shudder, he couldn't get over the fact that she had accessorized her ethnic lime green outfit with black shoes and a black handbag – that's a major fashion faux pas according to him – and he made it clear that he thought that those NGO types who only drank cheap Indian rum on the rocks were ridiculously self-righteous and insufferable. This was my cue to agree with him and I was angry enough with her to do it, but I couldn't. The truth is, I wanted to slap Ravi instead. Really whip him with my wide cobalt blue belt that went so outrageously well with my LBD – I mean, he was trashing my best friend! So when he attempted to kiss me as I slid out of the car, I sneakily turned my face around to ensure that he only got my ear. Oh bloody bloody god, I frantically thought to myself in the elevator, I hope I'd remembered to dab perfume behind my ears in the office loo that evening. I mean, so what if he was an ass – I still wanted him to go home fantasizing about me!

11.15 pm: I felt so guilty for not standing up for Ambika when Ravi made those rubbishy remarks about her that I called her while I was impatiently kicking off my shoes. 'Sorry,' I said breathlessly, 'I was in the lift when you called.' Ambika said no, no, it was she who was sorry – so very, very, very sorry for being nasty to Ravi the night before. I told her to forget it, I was considering dumping him anyway. She demanded an explanation and I informed her that it was his idiotic boss fetish that put me off – I couldn't tell her the whole truth and make her feel bad, right? Ambika cut me short by shrieking, 'Bloody hell! That's exactly the reason why I couldn't stand him. He's such a boss sucker-upper!' Then both of us giggled over Ravi's frequent boss-related remarks that had peppered the conversation the night before. The ass said he read Ayn Rand's *The Fountainhead* because his boss told him that that book had changed his life forever, and that he watched the BBC regularly to cultivate a Brit accent because his boss said it never fails to impress clients.

12.05 am: I snuggled into bed with Ambika's words ringing in my head: 'Glad you decided to dump him; he loves his boss more than he could ever love a woman.' I really was glad I had decided to eject that eejit out of my life.

Thursday

9.00 am: Ravi called. I ignored it.

1.05 pm: Got a text message from Ravi: 'Are we on for tonight?' I sent a terse reply: 'Can't. Have to burn the midnight oil reading *The Best of Calvin & Hobbes* because my boss says it changed the way she looks at other people's lives.' I smirked as I sent that message.

9.30 pm: Mentally kicked self for not agreeing to meet Ravi. There are only boring re-runs on TV. Heck, by now I know the dialogues of *The Big Bang Theory* by heart! Called Ambika but she's busy socializing with sex workers at an AIDS symposium. Asked her if we could meet tomorrow night, but she said she's going to spend the weekend in the interiors of Maharashtra with even more sex workers. 'At least one of us has something to do with sex,' I said wistfully and hung up.

9.41 pm: Was so, so bored, I felt myself weakening further. Fondly recalled the electricity bolt I felt when Ravi squeezed my hand, and sighed lustily. Have decided that it's no big deal if he's a pathetic ass-licker – at least he's a hot-looking pathetic ass-licker. You can't get everything, see?

9.48 pm: Called Ravi. Got a date tomorrow night, hooray!

Friday

11.45 am: Snuck out of office way before lunch

break for waxing, threading, blast dry, et cetera. I'm going to blow him away tonight.
8.40 pm: Ravi had ghastly fuzz on his face! Said his boss told him that people will take him more seriously if he has a beard. Was slightly put off, but all that changed when he held my hand. Am wondering now that if Benjamin Franklin had put Ravi on a kite string instead of a key, would there have been a bigger flash of lightning?

Saturday

3 pm: Woke up in Ravi's arms. Never got out of bed till he left.

Sunday

10.15 pm: Ambika called. Guiltily told her that I have changed my mind about Ravi and we are now officially an item. There was a long pause, broken only by a soft sigh from Ambika. It could have been a groan. I hastily mumbled that apart from his boss fetish, Ravi is quite a wonderful guy.

'In bed, I'm assuming,' Ambika said dryly.

'That also,' I graciously conceded.

Then I begged Ambika to be nice to him and she frostily said she would try, for my sake.

I needed more enthusiasm from her so I airily told her that Ravi's boss was majorly into charity events. I wasn't lying, exactly – Ravi had mentioned that his boss had attended a charity dinner a year ago and got Richard Gere's autograph which was framed and hung in his office cabin and probably dusted lovingly every day.

'Well, if he's willing to actually donate vast sums of his corporate funds to my NGO, I can help him collect autographs of even more celebs. Bill Gates and Warren Buffet too, perhaps. Work on that, will you?' Ambika said, sounding a little more amenable.

'Bill Gates and Warren Buffet? Really?' I squeaked.

'Um, well, we live in hope – look, it's mainly sex workers but you don't have to tell him that,' was Ambika's cheerful reply.

11 pm: Called Ravi. Had to con him into liking Ambika so I first gushed on and on and on about what a fabulous social life those NGO types led. Told him that Ambika was on first-name terms with Richard, Bill and Warren; I deliberately did not mention Dolly, Baby, etc. Then I casually asked if his boss would be interested in attending high-profile charity events. I got him there! He said he's going to try to set up a meeting between Ambika and his boss. Am keeping my fingers crossed. It's very important to me that Ambika and Ravi get along.

Monday

12.35 pm: Ravi called. He said Ambika could come to his office at 5 pm. He sounded like an excited little boy who had got five gold stars and a pat on the back from his teacher.
12.36 pm: Called Ambika and told her. She whooped with joy.
7.30 pm: Doodling impatiently while waiting for Ambika and Ravi at the pub. Wow, they're walking in together now and chatting like old buddies.
12.20 am: Well, well. The meeting was a huge success – it turned out that Ravi's boss knew Ambika's dad! It gets even better – Ambika's dad was his mentor and he still worships him. Ambika had the grace to blush when Ravi gushed about how his boss said Ambika's dad was the person who had urged him to read *The Fountainhead*, the book that had changed his life! I had to suppress a smirk. When Ravi popped into the loo I whispered to Ambika, 'So now it doesn't matter if you introduce his boss to Dolly and Baby instead of Bill and Warren, is it?' She nodded her head, and her smile was so wide you could fit a sofa length-wise into it.

The evening was great fun and I didn't feel a twinge of disappointment when Ravi dropped me home first since Ambika lives closer to him. It's so lovely when best friends and boyfriends get along famously!

Tuesday

8 pm: Went to the pub with Ravi – and Ambika! I hadn't invited her, so I guess he had. We had great fun once again but I did feel a little disappointed when he dropped me home first again. Whine, moan. I could have done with a little cuddle, at the very least!

Wednesday

6.30 pm: Am home and alone. All alone. Ravi's boss has taken Ambika and Ravi to dinner at a fab new lounge bar.
11 pm: It's no fun watching re-runs of *Castle* – I already know whodunit, dammit!
12.30 am: Sent Ravi a text message. He didn't bother to answer. Sent one to Ambika as well. She didn't bother to answer either! Sent another urgent message to Ambika: *Call wen home!!!!!!*

Thursday

7.30 am: Really annoyed that Ambika did not follow my 'Call wen home' instructions last night. I called her as soon as I woke up and she sleepily moaned that she'd call me later. 'Have a mother of a hangover,' she mumbled and disconnected the call. I called Ravi – he didn't bother to answer his phone.

11.30 am: Ravi finally called, thank god! He sounded as hungover as Ambika. I asked him how last night was in a brittle voice, and he told me it was 'fucking amazing' with a laugh but said he was too busy to furnish details. Asked him where we were meeting tonight and he said that he was in no shape to go out. All he wanted was his bed as soon as the day was done. 'How about my bed?' I offered in a husky voice. Damn, I never ever thought that I would be fobbed off with a 'Not tonight darling, I have a hangover' excuse! Am now ready to throw a tantrum.

8 pm: Called Ambika – she still hasn't given me the lowdown on her outing with Ravi and his boss. Her phone is switched off.

11.30 pm: Ambika's phone is still switched off. Gosh, wonder how much they drank last night!

Friday

5.30 pm: Was in a state of panic all day because Ravi didn't call. Finally swallowed my pride and called him in the evening. He answered the phone after about seventeen persistent rings! He says he can't meet me this entire weekend and mumbled something about being busy with old school friends. Was very miffed. I immediately called Ambika on a hunch and she warily said that she was going to the interiors of Maharashtra again. 'With sex workers or for sex?' I said waspishly and disconnected the call before she could reply. Sometimes I don't want to hear the truth, okay? Damn! Double damn! Triple damn! I will never ever encourage my next best friend to get chummy with my next boyfriend!

3

Diet Wars

11th April

Have discovered comfy XXXL clothes! Stepped into a mum & baby care store to buy a pressie for Anu's baby and saw fab super-stretch trousers. My tummy can finally breathe, hooray! Rushed to the changing room with thirteen clothes, at least. Skinny Salesgirl was v. annoying, though. She smiled widely and asked how many months preggers I was. Did not want to embarrass self so lied and said seven months. She gasped and said I looked ready to pop, was I going to have twins? Pretended I was deaf and sailed to the billing counter with my purchases. Nasty Skinny Salesgirl followed and asked if I'd like nursing bras as well. Eeeeeeee! I could have hit her! Was in such a hurry to get away from her, I forgot to buy the pressie for Anu's baby after all. Damn.

Will have to give Anu's baby money in a pale blue envelope instead.

Nasty Skinny Salesgirl's rude remarks rankled. Grimly decided on a strict fruit diet. Consumed four bananas, six mangoes and six chikoos for lunch and dinner. Halo shining. Can't wait to check my weight tomorrow morning! Am now feeling more charitable towards Nasty Skinny Salesgirl – because of her I am finally motivated to lose weight and perhaps I'll get my job at the airline back. Am still seething with rage that Bubbles and I were suspended three months ago for being fat. It's all their fault – who asked them to put us in charge of business class with all that lovely goose liver pâté, caviar and those sinfully creamy desserts just lying around!

12th April

Help! Weighed self and almost wept – am now one kg heavier than yesterday! Bloody diets don't work, that's what! Called Bubbles and whined. She sneered and said I ate the wrong fruit – mango, chikoo and banana are sugar-rich and I should have eaten watermelon instead. Don't think I like Bubbles v. much any more. Think she patronizes me because she weighs just sixty-nine kg. Shan't hang out with her in future.

Was so depressed, I decided to have a diet club sandwich *without* bread for brekker: ham, bacon, cheese, half-fried egg, lettuce, tomato and cucumber. To make it exciting, had low-fat chips with it. I boiled the potatoes first, then cut them into thick slices and lightly fried them in a non-stick pan. Yum! Maybe I can write a diet cookbook called *The Tasty Way to Lose Weight*, and become a famous Bollywood dietician. I will be rich, rich, rich! So rich that I can buy that mum & baby care store and sack Nasty Skinny Salesgirl! And I will never have to stand on a weighing scale in the airline office and be humiliated again.

21st April

Bloody bloody diets don't bloody work! Been starving self on breadless club sandwiches and chips and have put on even more weight. If Nasty Skinny Salesgirl sees me now bet she'll want to know if I'm having triplets! Hate everybody, esp. Bubbles. She called yesterday to say she's on a new diet and has lost two kg in three days. Showoff! Know that she's *dying* for me to ask for the diet, but won't give her the satisfaction. She laughed meanly when I told her about my low-fat chips and said even monkeys know that carbs are a big no-no. Will go for a one-hour walk in the evenings and lose more weight than her, so there! I'll show her!

Can't sleep. Tormented by the thought that if Bubbles continues to lose weight she will start flying again and I will have to settle for a lowly ground job at the airport. OMG, I'll have to duck if I see her on duty!

22nd April

Could not bring self to go for a walk today. Too hot. Put AC on in living room and decided to walk up and down like a caged tiger through an entire episode of a cooking prog., *Jamie at Home*, and succeeded, yay! Ran up and down for a few rounds as well but had to stop because neighbour in flat below intercommed and screamed that I'd ruined her afternoon nap: she sternly reminded me that we are not permitted to shift heavy furniture between 2 and 4 pm and has threatened to complain to the building society secretary. Told her to go to hell!

Felt much thinner and decided to treat self to what

Jamie was cooking: chicken in a cheesy sauce. Had to have an extra helping because I virtuously decided not to mop up the cheese sauce with carbs. Bubbles called and wanted to come over to show her new thin self off: she says her tummy is one inch thinner. Coldly told her I was going out. Do not wish to associate with showoffs. Cannot believe that I used to beg the rostering dept. to put us on the same flight together!

29th April

Have stopped taking calls from Bubbles altogether. She can't take a hint, though. Has started sending me text messages about her new weight: acc. to the latest one, she now weighs 66.8 kg. She wants to know if we can go out to celebrate. Will not respond. Am in despair, though. My weight-loss pacing sessions with Jamie Oliver on TV are not working. Looking at all that lovely food inspires me to cook it too. Haven't lost an ounce. Think perhaps I have a thyroid problem. Called friendly neighbourhood doc for details on thyroid test. V. easy, just a blood test. Will do it first thing tom.

2nd May

Gloom and doom. Got thyroid test report. My thyroid is fine, damn. Friendly neighbourhood doc is not v. friendly, though. She says I should go on a strict diet and exercise daily. Told her I already am, and she scoffed when I gave her the details. Told me to stick to watermelon for a week and walk in the park for an hour in the morning and an hour in the evening – at least. Did not like her tone of voice. Hate everybody, esp. Bubbles. Her latest text msg. says she now weighs 65.6 kg. If she carries on like this, she'll be back at the airline within a month. Cretin!

3rd May

Tried watermelon diet for half a day and felt dizzy and sick. Lay on bed and weakly called the pizza joint next door. Ordered a small pepperoni pizza and then had to order a large one an hour later. Feeling slightly better now. Diets make me ill.

7th May

There's hope yet! Today's newspaper carried an article about a lady with an eight-kg cyst in her stomach. She was successfully operated on and is eight kg lighter in less than two days! Am certain I have a cyst too that weighs about twenty-two kg. That's why diets and exercise don't work for me. Will fix apt. with doc – not the unfriendly neighbourhood doc but another one. After surgery,

I will take Bubbles's calls and invite her over to see my new body. Will prob. weigh fifty kg then, yay! And fly before she can, double yay!

11th May

New doc v. warm and sympathetic. She said I must certainly do an ultrasound and recommended a few more tests as well at her husband's clinic.

13th May

The ultrasound was horrible. Was made to drink gallons of water and not allowed to pee till the examination was over. Asked sourpuss technician if she could see the cyst but she refused to tell me. Said I must wait for the report tom. Had to pay a hefty sum (now twenty-five grand poorer) but who cares? I will be thin and sexy!

Treated self to biryani and gelato. Have to be strong for cyst surgery. Got new text msg. from Bubbles. Says she's now 64.9 kg. Hah! Wait till my surgery is over. Then we'll talk!

14th May

Sympathetic new doc even more sympathetic now. She says there's no cyst (boo hoo), but has recommended bariatric surgery at her brother-in-law's nursing home. Almost fainted when she told me how much it costs. Told her I'd think about it. V. depressed. Had fifty-five panipuris to feel better. Noticed that the panipuri man has a bad cold and uses the same dirty cloth to blow his nose and wipe his hands with. Don't care. Maybe I'll get his germs, fall ill and lose weight. Or maybe I'll get worms from eating unsanitary roadside food and they'll eat my weight away. Am desperate now. Read in the papers that even Nigella Lawson is on a diet – I will be the only tubby person left on earth!

Bubbles called eleven times today. Ignored all her calls. She sent twenty text msgs. too, begging me to see her. Says she's v. ill, possibly dying. I ignored her text msgs. Hah! This is just a ruse to get me to view and envy her new 63.7 kg body. People can be so slimy.

17th May

Bubbles called at least fifty times today. Lost count after a while. Ignored her calls, naturally.

21st May

Am in shock! Read newspaper article today that says that people put on truckloads of weight if their friends are fat! Now all my friends will avoid me like the plague and nobody, not even strangers, will talk to me ever again for fear of becoming obese through association! Hell, even Bubbles will give me a wide berth! I will die alone and friendless! Maybe I'll have to rob a bank and have that shockingly expensive bariatric surgery, after all. Called mum to ask for an advance on my inheritance. She turned down my request – said all I need is self-control to lose weight, not money, particularly not *her* precious money. Hung up quickly before she could begin her usual boring lecture on moderation.

22nd May

Whew! Bubbles called this morning, and this time I answered the phone at the first ring. Am relieved to have at least one friend in the world. She cried and cried and cried. Says she is almost bald – her new diet has made her hair fall in clumps. The only airline that may hire her now is the no-frills, buy-your-own-meals one where retro wigs are part of the dress code for stewardesses. OMG, she'll have to buy her own sandwiches when on duty! Rushed to meet her. God, she looked thin but awful. We both agreed that diets are silly and we are happier being fat. We called the airline and asked if they had any openings for ground staff. Have to fill application forms tomorrow. Then we ordered pepperoni pizzas to feel better – four large ones to help Bubbles's hair grow back faster. Told her about the mum & baby care store's roomy pregnancy clothes and we're going to go there soon. Will just have to tell Nasty Skinny Salesgirl that the twins were safely delivered and am pregnant again.

4

Au Revoir

I'm doing the night shift at the hospital – both R and I begged her family for it. They relented with understandable reluctance; since the countdown has begun, every moment now is precious. The nurse puts her finger on her lips in a bossy, class-monitor way to warn me that R is sleeping. I tip-toe into the room and anxiously scan her face – she looks so peaceful, it makes my blood run cold. I check her pulse and am reassured. Then I drag a chair to the window, take out a pen and writing pad and pour my scrambled thoughts out on paper. I stopped bringing books with me because I just couldn't concentrate. Perhaps I was destined to be the recorder of R's last days on earth – while she's dying I shall be killing time. 'Days not weeks, sorry,' the doctor had told us last evening with an apologetic shrug, and I had squeezed her sister's limp, damp hand with my equally limp and damp hand.

Tonight I notice that all the spine-chilling tubes

are out. R is back to being her hands-free version again.

I hear R cough and look up from my scribbling. Her eyes are wide open and she's regarding me anxiously.

'Did you get it?' she asks eagerly.

'What do you think?' I hiss and rummage through my large bag. 'One bottle of rum, a thermos packed with ice cubes, wedges of lime and soda for you, and cola for me coming up. Thank god you don't smoke or I'd be hauled out of here on my arse.' I take everything out, including a pair of crystal glasses, and play cocktail waitress.

R props herself up on her pillows and raises her eyebrows at the glasses. 'Nice touch,' she says appreciatively. 'I was worried that you'd bring ugly steel glasses like the ones in which we were furtively served alcohol at that grungy seafood restaurant on dry days.' She scrunches her brow helplessly.

'I've forgotten the name of that restaurant,' she wails. She looks distressed.

'So have I,' I say brusquely. 'And I've also forgotten the name of the guy you used to date then, fortunately.'

R's distressed look vanishes. She laughs. 'He was such an ass.'

I hand her the drink and we clink glasses.

'To all the asses in our lives,' I say solemnly. And then I mentally kick myself for using the word 'lives'. That was clumsy of me.

R takes a tiny sip and grimaces. I jump to my feet and whip out her bedpan in case she's going to throw up. False alarm.

'If you bring that smelly thing even an inch closer to me, I shall throw up all over you,' R says severely.

I park myself in my chair but R makes me leap up again.

'Give me that bag,' she says imperiously and points to a purple polka-dotted toilet bag on a little cabinet.

I obediently do her bidding and she unzips the bag and hands me a tiny bottle of hand sanitizer. I don't bother to hide a smirk and make a mental note to toss this little bottle into R's funeral pyre. For as long as I've known her, she wouldn't step out of her apartment without one of these bottles. I squeeze some on my palms and rub my hands briskly while R watches me like a hawk.

R takes another sip, a larger one this time, and sighs, 'Heaven.'

I wince. I've become very sensitive to certain words.

I take a huge gulp, she does likewise and within minutes I'm pouring another couple of drinks.

'Could you be a little more generous with my rum?' R says belligerently.

I'm torn.

'Look, it will make you feel sick,' I feebly say.

R laughs mirthlessly.

'Rubbish. This is the best medicine I've had over the past few months. I feel better already!'

She really does look better. More animated, and the sparkle is back in her eyes.

Hallelujah, the buzz is on like before. All that's missing is Alannah Myles belting out 'Black Velvet' or Don McLean's 'American Pie', R's favourite songs. I've already compiled a list of songs in my head that I associate with R – I have a feeling I'll be listening to them on a loop when I feel lonely.

'Back to that ass I used to date during the grungy seafood-restaurant days,' R says. 'I can't believe what I ever saw in him. Did I tell you he once asked if we were lesbians?'

I can feel myself blinking. 'He what?'

R grins. 'Look, we do everything together. I think he kind of hoped.' She leaves it at that with a giggle.

I snort. 'Thank god he's over. I just loved the expression on his face when you sent me to his office with his things carelessly tossed into a cardboard box. It was a very heavy box – I wish

I'd thrown it at him,' I say viciously. And I do feel vicious. I want to kill everyone who hadn't been nice to R. Including myself. I hadn't been a good enough friend often. Particularly during the time I was dating someone who made her hackles rise. He couldn't stand her frequent put-me-downs either, so R and I barely met those days. That was mean of me – I had let my fickle hormones come in the way of friendship.

I clearly remember, when that relationship was over, I had sent R over to his house with his things stuffed into a torn sports bag. In the course of our long friendship, both of us had played courier girls for each other.

Tears sting my eyes when I realize that after R goes I'll have no one to deliver the debris of relationships to exes. I attempt to squeeze the tears back into my eyes – I feel myself failing, but I'm saved by the clickety-clack of approaching hospital regulation kitten-heel shoes for nurses in the corridor. My alarm is reflected in R's eyes and I spring up, delve into my voluminous bag and spray the room with air freshener. The rank smell of rum cowers beneath a lively lemony fragrance. I specifically chose citrus for this evening. The heavy scent of flowers always reminds me of death.

Both of us heave audible sighs of relief as the footsteps fade away.

R clutches the spot where her heart is. 'I almost died!' she gasps, and cackles meanly when she sees me flinch at her words.

'Stop pussyfooting around me,' she says, exasperated. 'So I'm dying, deal with it. I'd really appreciate it if you could put off the mourning till later. Like, when I'm not here to see that hangdog expression on your face any more. It doesn't suit you and it's beginning to annoy me.'

The drink has got to R and I quickly pour myself an extra-large shot to join her where she's at. I down it in one gulp, and fix myself another. I'm almost there!

'When you do meet God, would you ask him to find a nice guy for me?' I implore, valiantly attempting to lighten the atmosphere.

'Sure, what kind of man?' R says expansively.

I think hard and come up with what, in my drunken haze, I think is a gem.

'A man who is not embarrassed to hold my handbag when I visit a public loo – even if it's bright pink,' I say excitedly.

R applauds.

'That's more profound than that dreadful Paulo effing Coelho,' she says.

'So do you finally believe in God?' I ask. I have to know. We're both rabid atheists. Has this changed her mind?

R indignantly chokes on her drink and I gently rub her back. If she hadn't been sick I'd have thumped it hard.

'I'll tell you this – if there is a god, and that idiotic god person expects me to kiss his feet and play the harp for him, I'll strangle him with a harp string,' she spits out savagely.

'You go girl, I'm with you!' I say.

'Do you think I really care about dying? I mean, how wonderful has my life been that I want it to go on forever? My life has been effing mediocre. And so has yours,' she adds.

True. I nod. 'And you'll be spared wrinkles, the scraggy chicken neck, the sickening crunch as your head hits a glass ceiling and more loser boyfriends,' I say wistfully. I've reached the stage where I want to be in her shoes. Really. I'm the one who's going to be suffering, left behind on Earth without my best friend. Tears rush to my eyes – and this time they're for me and me alone.

'You're crying,' R says accusingly like I'm a party pooper. 'When you're done, can you fix me another?'

I fix myself another as well.

'Promise me one thing,' R says. Her words are becoming slurred.

'Of course, anything,' I say. I expect her to tell me where she wants part of her ashes scattered, what charities I should give her clothes and books to and things like that.

Instead, R says, 'If I survive tonight, can we do this again tomorrow? With G & Ts instead of rum? And only Schweppes, not that dreadful Indian cat's piss masquerading as tonic, okay?'

'Promise,' I cross my heart dramatically.

'I want music too,' R says petulantly, 'and you know what, I want it now!'

She picks up the TV remote and goes to VH1. It's classic rock hour, Tears for Fears are doing their 'Shout, shout, let it all out' routine and R increases the volume. She shouts along with them, letting it all out. I've never seen her this angry.

I panic. 'Turn it off!' I say, but R ignores me and makes it louder.

Even through the deafening decibel levels I can hear an army of kitten heels racing towards her room. I debate between lunging for the remote or the air freshener. The air freshener wins but this time the rank fumes of rum stubbornly refuse to give way to citrus.

Several irate nurses barge in. I think I'm having a

heart attack and I swear to myself that I will strangle God with a harp string before R gets there. I black out.

When I come to, I'm lying on R's bed and she's slumped on the chair.

'Oh good, you're up,' she says, looking cheerful.

'What happened?' I ask. I'm still feeling bemused.

She waves a hospital receipt in her hand. 'I've been expelled from the hospital,' she gloats and giggles.

I sit up with a start.

'Oh god, I shouldn't have brought the alcohol, I'm so sorry,' I groan.

'What? Are you crazy? This is the only way to go!' she grins. She looks exultant.

I drop R home. I'm embarrassed about what happened, but her family seems very amused, even proud of R's spunky expulsion when she insists that she had bludgeoned me into sneaking alcohol into the hospital. At this stage, more than the breath, it's the spirit that counts. We all wordlessly agree that it's nice to see her so alive.

R and I have the G & T bash the next evening. I have bought a bottle of the finest imported gin available at my neighbourhood alcohol shop and I fling roughly half into the funeral pyre. I quickly follow this up with a can of Schweppes and the flames suddenly rise sky high and merge with the setting sun. All the mourners look up, astonished. I clap my hands over my mouth so no one can tell I'm laughing. Trust R to do a crazy pyrotechnic farewell – she always was a bit of a show-off.

I drink the other half of the bottle at home later, with a silly smile on my face. I wonder if she's strangling God and I hope he cries.

It's raining now. Unseasonal rain that's gushing and pouring relentlessly. I hear a clattering noise – I rush to the window to see kamikaze hailstones smashing themselves to smithereens on the pavement. I hold my glass out to collect a few hailstones and pour some G & T in.

Yep, she's made the bastard weep.

5

Wannabe Mum

Friday night

Saw Altaf at a bookshop today. I don't think he noticed me, whew. I ducked hastily behind a shelf of recipe books and practically crawled out of the bookshop on all fours, my cheeks burning from the curious and/or amused stares of fellow book browsers. It's been over three months since Altaf and I parted ways – if we'd been married our divorce papers would cite irreconcilable differences: I badly wanted a baby, he firmly didn't, end of beautiful love story. Seeing him brought back the desire for both Altaf and a baby, sigh. Am now experiencing a sharp pang of longing in my gut and a sharper pain in my lower back. Am too old to make sudden, jerky movements like ducking to avoid exes. And if I don't find a man soon, I'll be too old to have a baby as well. Am thirty-four plus, ouch! That hurts more than my back.

Am now lying in bed with a box of assorted chocs, my laptop on my tummy and lashings of muscle-spasm ointment slathered on my back. Nisha had popped in with the ointment. She said it's so fantastic, by tomorrow morning I'll be able to twirl hula hoops around my waist without wincing. Oh, it's wonderful to have an old friend as a neighbour! Ever since Nisha moved in with her family last month, my life as a single woman has become more balanced. No more spending dateless weekends pining alone – she usually pops in to escape from what she calls the humdrum of catering to the needs of her husband and two-year-old son. My problem is, after Altaf, I haven't met anyone I'd like to share breakfast in bed with, leave alone a baby! They all fall short.

Saturday afternoon

Woke up in the morning feeling fab and thinking positive. Did not try that hula-hoop thingie, though, mainly because I do not own a hula hoop. When Nisha popped in at noon to check on me, I excitedly told her the idea I'd been tossing around my head all night: I was going to adopt a baby and be a single mum!

Was very disappointed that Nisha did not share my enthusiasm. She scoffed at me instead and demanded to know who would look after the child while I was at work. I weakly mumbled 'Crèche' and she sniffed and said, 'And what about when you travel?' I was silent because my job takes me all over the country every month. I have earned enough air miles to get a free round-the-world ticket! Nisha broke the silence first and warned me not to even consider her for the post because as soon as her son started proper school she was going to get a part-time job and spend quality time with adults.

'Don't worry, I wasn't even thinking of asking you,' I said frostily. That was a big fat lie because I was kind of hoping that she'd willingly pitch in.

'Good,' Nisha said in a hard voice, and added that unless I was an obscenely wealthy celeb-type person with an army of servants, there was no way I could bring up a child alone. She also asked me with a sneer if I fancied myself as India's answer to Angelina Jolie in her pre-Brad Pitt days. I lost it and hotly told her that I wasn't planning to adopt children from every single continent on planet Earth, thank you very much. More nasty words were exchanged when Nisha condescendingly told me that bringing up a child isn't child's play and that I was foolishly romanticizing the notion. Nisha eventually stormed out and I was hugely glad when I heard the door slam. I mean, no wonder we hadn't been best friends in college – we were merely part of a large gang of backbenchers.

Now wondering how I can keep my job and bring up a baby. I can't do this after I retire or both the baby and I would be wearing incontinence diapers at the same time!

Saturday evening

Ha ha, Fate really is a bitch goddess! Nisha's husband called and tentatively asked if I could look after their two-year-old for a few hours tonight because there was a movie they desperately wanted to watch. I agreed readily, gloating over the fact that this would show Nisha that I wasn't as selfish as her and she would owe me big time. Perhaps she would meekly offer to look after my baby when I travelled, after this! I asked him if I could speak to Nisha but he warily said she was in the loo. 'Ask her to call me when she's out,' I insisted. There was no way I was going to give up my chance to gloat and make Nisha grovel!

Called the neighbourhood store and ordered chocolate, biscuits, ice cream, cheese slices, chips, microwave popcorn and all the yummy things kids like. Apart from the opportunity of making Nisha eat crow, I was rather excited about looking after her baby. I could play mommy for a few hours, hooray!

Saturday night

Am writing this sitting on an upturned bucket in the loo while the little darling is doing potty. Nisha the coward didn't call or even drop her son to my flat. Her husband rang the doorbell with the kid and handed me a bag the size of a family suitcase. I asked if his son was going to live with me forever and Nisha's husband grinned. He's a really cool guy, he deserves someone nicer than her! To his astonishment, the kid didn't weep and wail at the prospect of being left alone with me – he said he was looking forward to it. Love the little angel – he's definitely taken after his dad! I was given a tiffin box with his dinner too. Told Nisha's husband that I had planned to order pizza for the kid and he wrinkled his nose. He said Nisha's very firm that he eats fresh homemade food only. Gawd, she's such a bore.

'By the way, where's Nisha?' I asked pointedly, and her husband looked guilty. He gazed at his feet and stuttered that she was in the loo. I squawked, 'Still?' Then I looked concerned and gently pointed out that it wasn't advisable to take her out for a movie if she had the runs. Nisha's husband squirmed and mumbled some unintelligible rubbish. He squirmed yet again when I handed him a strip of Imodium to stop Nisha's pretend runs and sweetly asked him to give it to Nisha. If I'd had the time I'd have made a sarcastic get-well-soon card for her too!

Uh oh, the angel's done with his potty and demands that I scrub his botty. Good lord, the loo is reeking!

Saturday night – a little later

As I lovingly washed, dried and powdered the little darling, I discovered that nothing on Earth smells as delicious as a powdered baby bottom! Couldn't resist planting several kisses there. Threatened to eat his bottom and the angel giggled and squealed.

Then I put him on my lap, wrapped my arms tightly around him, and we watched cartoons back to back on TV. I laughed the loudest when the sweetheart demanded an apple because a cartoon dragon was eating one! Kids are so darn cute. During ad breaks we chatted about what he's going to be when he grows up. He says he's going to be a robber because that way he can get anything he wants without going to office and working hard like his daddy. He also told me his daddy calls his boss very, very bad names. And then the cartoons were back on and he laughed so hard at the antics of a panther on a skateboard, that some of his pee accidently fell into his pants and onto my pristine white kurta!

Naturally, the kid had to be washed and changed yet again. Am now beginning to understand why Nisha packed six pairs of shorts and underpants for just a few hours – wish she had included a few plastic sheets in the suitcase as well. That was very thoughtless of her! Inhaled his bottom deeply after dusting it with powder but was too tired to kiss it. Changed my damp clothes as well and my heart sank when I noticed a deep yellow stain on my kurta. I have firmly resolved to wear only dark colours when I have my own baby.

Cannot watch cartoons any more. Those squeaky voices are beginning to grate on my nerves. This time round, I have the laptop on my lap instead of the kid. Just in case.

Saturday night – much later

Am so exhausted I could die! Had to chase the brat around the house with his mother's specially packed dinner which he kept spitting out. Cockroaches will have a party in my flat tonight, of that I'm certain. Finally lost my patience when he flung his bowl of watery dal and rice onto my expensive pale blue rug and shouted at him. He burst into loud, eardrum-shattering tears, demanding his mommy and daddy, and still hasn't stopped. Tried to console him in vain – he starts screaming when I attempt to put my arms around him. I've changed my mind – the brat has taken after his annoying mother. All I can do now is sit and wait out his tantrum.

Saturday night – much, much later

The brat is sleeping, whew. He stopped wailing after I offered to tell him a story and allowed me to lead him to my bed, still sniffling. He took out his Bob the Builder pajamas from his suitcase and handed them to me. I changed him and tucked him into bed. He looked so innocent and angelic sucking his thumb that I couldn't resist running my fingers through his satiny hair. My yearning for a baby surged to an all-time high. Then I started telling him a story about Cinderella, and he suddenly screamed that he didn't want a silly old girl's story, he only wanted a Bob the Builder story! When I apologetically told him that I didn't know any Bob the Builder stories he started crying for his mommy and daddy again! Nothing I said or did could console him, and eventually he cried himself to sleep. Have decided that I only want a baby girl now. Boys are horrors.

Saturday night – much, much, much later

Cannot wait for the brat's parents to pick him up – want my flat to myself again! Am feeling as indignant as the three bears when they discovered that Goldilocks broke into their house and made a right mess of it. Baby Bear's piteous line, 'Someone is sleeping on my bed!' is playing in my head.

Saturday night – much, much, much, much later

The horror's dad picked him up and thanked me profusely for looking after his offspring as he carried him out in his arms. I nodded weakly. Did not have the energy to warmly say, 'You're welcome to leave him here any time.' Also, am not a liar. Looked at the mess my flat was in after I locked the front door and decided that I'd deal with it the next day.

Sunday afternoon

Slept very badly because specks of that infernal baby talc still lingered in the air and tickled my throat. It didn't help that the doorbell rang at 6.30 am. Ignored it and buried my face in my pillow. Doorbell rang again and again and again so I was forced to drag myself out of bed and shuffle to the door. It was Nisha's husband looking hugely apologetic and the devil's spawn looking anxious! The horror had left his dinky ambulance behind, apparently. Sleepily slumped self into a chair while Nisha's husband and the brat checked under furniture for the dinky ambulance. Was too tired to worry if my nightie was transparent. The pest started crying when they couldn't find it and had to be dragged screaming and kicking out of my flat by his dad.

I found the dinky ambulance five minutes after they left – I tripped on it and went flying in the air. I stubbed my toe when I landed and sharp, shooting pains started emanating from my back all over again. I did not call Nisha's husband to inform him that the dinky ambulance was discovered. Frankly, I didn't care! I tumbled into bed with a groan instead.

When I woke up at 2 pm, I sent a text message to Altaf, informing him that my biological clock had stopped ticking and I wanted babies as desperately as dogs want fleas. Am now waiting with bated breath for his response.

Sunday evening

Spent an agonizing thirty minutes waiting for Altaf to say something, anything! Pictured him in bed with another woman and sneering at my text message. When he finally did get back, the message was terse: 'What time can I pick you up?' Am now dressed and ready an hour in advance!

I rushed to the mirror to take one last frantic look at my face when the doorbell rang. I needn't have bothered since it wasn't Altaf but a rather subdued and embarrassed Nisha with a box of Lindt Orange Chocolate Thins (she remembered they were my favourite chocs!) instead. She thanked me profusely and I was in such in a good mood I didn't bother to gloat. Then she told me I was looking lovely and asked where I was going and, more importantly, whom I was looking like a supermodel for. I mumbled 'Altaf' and she looked astonished and blinked several times. Light gradually dawned in her eyes and she grinned. Then we both laughed so hard, tears poured down our cheeks. I had to re-do my eyeliner because it had smudged badly. Nisha's not a bad sort, really.

Monday dawn

Got home very, very late because Altaf drove around the city looking for a chocolate shop that was open after midnight. He said we owe Nisha's son big time and I couldn't agree more. Have been instructed to hand the chocolate over first thing tomorrow morning. Now waiting for Altaf to finish his shower and join me in bed. Thank god he's carrying protection in his wallet!

Not-so-grim Fairy Tales for Big, Bad Girls

1

The Princess and the Pea Pâté

Once upon a time there lived a not-so-handsome prince. Nevertheless, his wealth and power made him exceedingly attractive to women. He had an insatiable appetite and nibbled the ears and toes of *Playboy* centre-spreads, casting-couch starlets, barmaids and the odd scullery maid or two between meals. On his thirtieth birthday, the king demanded a legitimate heir to the throne, for a change. His mother's only stipulation was that she should be a blue-blooded princess.

An alliance was fixed with an English princess but the prince hastily backed out when he discovered that, if given a choice between the Marlboro man and his horse, she'd take the horse any day.

So he happily returned to his wild oats-sowing ways till on a dark and stormy night a young girl arrived at the castle. She introduced herself as a princess and said that her BMW had broken down.

Probably vulgar new money, the queen thought to herself with a shudder. The prince invited her to spend the night at the castle, preferably in his bedroom. The queen, however, would have none of it and strode off to prepare the guest room furthest from the prince's.

Now, instead of changing the sheets and putting fresh flowers in the vase, the queen did a very peculiar thing: she placed a frozen pea on a mattress and put seven thick mattresses on top. Thoughtfully placing a ladder next to it, she returned to find the prince looking interestedly down the alleged princess's cleavage.

Since it was the cook's night off, leftovers were on the menu. The alleged princess offered to prepare a four-course meal instead, in return for their kindness. The result was foodie heaven and the prince declared the rabbit vindaloo far better than the best orgasm he'd ever had. Then, to prove that he meant every word he said, he rolled over and went to sleep.

After dessert (a crumbly, melt-in-the-mouth apple pie), the queen personally escorted the alleged princess to her bedroom. The alleged princess thought the whole seven-mattress thing was rather odd but dismissed it as a quaint medieval custom and spent a very uncomfortable night indeed because the pea hurt so. The next morning, the queen was delighted to see raccoon-like dark circles under the alleged princess's eyes and bruises on her back and proclaimed her to be the real thing.

The princess was furious when she discovered that the queen had deliberately placed the pea there to find out if she was an imposter. 'Why not a simple DNA test?' she screamed. 'Or my passport or even an attested birth certificate instead of medieval torture?' She stalked out of the castle in search of a lawyer but the prince raced after her and calmed her down with a deeply satisfying CPR kiss.

And you can't get up till you finish your pea.

He was determined to marry her because he thought her chicken breasts were far more delectable than any of the breasts he'd previously tasted. He also swore that her pheasant dressing was far more orgasmic than his peasant undressings. She accepted his proposal on one condition: all the finger food he ate thereafter would have to be personally prepared by her. Rejoicing, he uncorked the champagne (which the princess served with caviar on wafer-thin melba toast and a top-secret herb).

They had a huge wedding for which the princess herself supervised the royal feast and served exotic fusion cuisine instead of the usual greasy fare. After a few years, she converted the banquet hall of the castle into a dead posh theme restaurant that became the rage with jaded film stars and nouveau riche culture vultures.

The prince lived happily ever after too, till he became obese and sued her for clogging his arteries with fatty deposits.

Moral: Rabbit vindaloo is far more tempting than a Playboy Bunny.

2

Cindy

Once upon a time, there lived a fetching young orphan called Cindy. She shared a home with her stepmother and stepsisters who were as nice to her as step-families can be. They made her give them room-service meals, sweep and swab till not a speck of dust was visible through a microscope and do the usual odd jobs like thread their moustaches, administer bikini waxes, et cetera. They even tried to make her give them Brazilian waxes but Cindy firmly drew the line at that.

One day, there was a flurry of excitement at home because the prince announced that the Ms Planet contest would be held in the castle's ballroom. Cindy so wanted to go instead of watching it on TV but her step-family laughed cruelly at her and said that servants were not invited. They went on a series of fad diets (Fit for Life, Herbal Life, General Motors, Atkins and South Beach, to name a few) to shed their excess pounds. Unfortunately, they weren't very successful, and on the night of the ball they had to squeeze themselves into their wildly expensive designer wear. One stepsister even ripped the bodice of her gown when she sneezed, and raved and ranted till Cindy hit upon the idea of putting it fashionably together with safety pins, just like a daring Versace original.

After they sailed out leaving behind wafts of heavy perfume, a sorely disappointed Cindy wept buckets (three-and-a-half, to be precise) till there was a knock at the door. She prayed that it would be her fairy godmother but it turned out to be a vacuum-cleaner salesman. Cindy got a flash of inspiration: she asked him for a free demo and got the house spick and span before her step-family returned. Then she packed him off and got ready for the Ms Planet ball.

Wearing a crisply starched apron over her sexy little black dress, she entered the palace through the backdoor and introduced herself as one of the cocktail waitresses on duty for the do. Armed with a tray of smoked oysters on crackers, she circled the crowd clockwise and anti-clockwise, taking great care to avoid her step-family. Several times she looked up to see the prince staring at her with great interest and felt her heartbeat accelerate madly.

After Cindy had completed a few rounds with her tray, the prince brazenly approached her and offered his services as her PR agent. He practically ordered her to participate in the contest since her body and her looks (in that order) made her a sure-fire winner. She eagerly agreed and was then escorted to the green room where international make-up artists, hairdressers and designers worked their magic.

Before she knew it, Cindy was onstage with the other pretty young things. She was a natural. Her sweeping and swabbing had toned every muscle in her body and the judges had to call in the riot police during the swimsuit round. But her biggest success occurred during the question round: when asked to name the person she admired most in the world, she promptly said it was Mr Clean, her favourite detergent mascot, because he got deep-rooted stains out of the fabric of the world.

There was a stunned silence and then everyone in the audience got to their feet and applauded because it was such a pleasant change from Mother Teresa and Mahatma Gandhi. The moment her name was announced as the winner, Cindy suddenly realized that she had left the iron on at home and rushed off the stage leaving one mock-alligator leather slipper behind in her haste, but no forwarding address.

The next day, all the papers on the planet had her on their covers. An international hunt was on. A leading designer shoe manufacturer even sponsored a 'Hunt the Owner of the Slipper' contest. The prince, however, decided to do a spot of detective work on his own. He went from door to door with the slipper, claiming that the person who fit into it would be richly rewarded.

Meanwhile, Cindy was being force-fed French fries, full-cream milk, cheese, chocolate, red meat and carbs by her step-family as punishment for participating in the contest and having such a beautiful body. The prince came knocking just as they were cramming a double cheeseburger down her throat. He instantly recognized her and rushed to her rescue by gallantly shoving his finger down her throat.

After ordering the step-family to mop up the mess on the carpet, he took Cindy's hand, gazed deeply into her eyes and said, 'I'd love to marry you.' Her eyes lit up till he added, 'But I'm gay and in love with a designer. All I can offer you is a contract as an international supermodel.' She accepted and became a rich and famous cover girl. Thereafter, she released a DVD called *The Household Chores Workout*, which knocked Jane Fonda, Cindy Crawford and has-been Bollywood stars off the top of the celebrity exercise charts and became even richer. So she lived happily ever after, dating Formula 1 drivers, Hollywood actors and ageing rock stars even though she couldn't marry her prince.

Moral: Not all princes become kings. Some become queens.

3

Red Robbing Hoodlum and Wolfgang

Once upon a time, Red Robbing Hoodlum went to visit her hypochondriac grandmother with a paper bag of drugged chocolate, hoping to make away with the family silver. On her way through the concrete jungle, she hitched a ride with Wolfgang, a greasy, leather-jacketed youth on his souped-up 1000cc Cruiser. Wolfgang thought her red gig was ultimately kinky and reasoned things out this way: any girl who visits her grandma wearing a hood when it isn't Halloween intends to trick for treats. He dropped her two blocks away from her grandmother's ritzy bungalow and vroomed his evil way to Grandma's house. A sophisticated brunette answered the door.

'Grandma?' he enquired tenderly, upon which she snapped, 'Malti to you,' and attempted to slam the door shut but didn't succeed due to advanced osteoporosis. Once in, Wolfgang whipped out a gun and snarled, 'I call the shots, sister!' He trussed Grandma up like a turkey and locked her in the closet. Then, donning her brunette wig and her sheerest baby-doll nightie, he hopped into bed with Grandma's well-thumbed bible: *The Intelligent Woman's Guide to Life without Sex*.

When the doorbell rang seconds later, he screeched in a high falsetto, 'Lift the latch and come in, dear.' Red Robbing Hoodlum gaily tripped in and exclaimed, 'Grandma, you look dreadful!' This insensitive remark deeply wounded Wolfgang, who had rather fancied himself in Grandma's attire. Indeed, it had inspired him enough to briefly contemplate a sex change. Swallowing his bile, he feebly mumbled, 'Yes, well, I'm not quite myself, dear.' Then, patting the bed, he said, 'But don't mind me, make yourself comfortable.' Red Robbing Hoodlum continued to stare at him, mesmerized, while squawking.

'Grandma, you've got hair on your chest!' she squealed.

'Oh pshaw girl, that's just a hormonal imbalance.'

'And, er, Grandma, you're stroking my knee!'

'Yes, well, I do get lonely sometimes.'

Red Robbing Hoodlum's eyes became rounder and rounder. She sensed that something was wrong and decided to cut out all preliminaries and put her plan into action immediately. 'Here, Grandma, Mother sent these for you,' she said and stuffed a handful of chocolate into Wolfgang's mouth before he could protest. He went out like a light. As Red Robbing Hoodlum leapt to the closet and unlocked it to steal the family silver and black money, a trussed-up Grandma shot out, fell on her like a dead weight and knocked her out cold.

Wolfgang opened his eyes at the crash and spat out the drug-enhanced chocolate, which he deliberately hadn't swallowed. He untied Grandma, looked searchingly into her eyes and said, 'Forgive me, I just wanted to check out that little hussy.' Then he held her hand and continued, 'Such an attractive, vulnerable lady, all alone in this palatial bungalow. Allow me to move in here and look after you.' He hastily added, 'Alternatively, you could shift into my homely paying-guest digs, but I'd hate to uproot you,' and chucked Grandma under her chin.

Upon which Grandma simpered, 'I don't know, Wolfgang, the milkman might get jealous.'

Just then Red Robbing Hoodlum came to. She tossed back her hair and screeched, 'Grandma, beware of Wolf–'

Her voice stilled as a shot rang out and Wolfgang, replacing his gun, cried out her obituary, 'Even if you're winsome, you lose some, pigeon.'

Dear Agony Aunt,
Is it wise to try a 69 when you're 69?
Regards,
xxx

With that out of the way, he put his arms around Grandma and huskily said, 'Malti baby, wouldn't you like to produce a music video with me as the hero?'

Moral: If you're old and lonely, ditch being coy – get yourself a sexy toy boy.

4

I Kissed a Frog

Once upon a time there was a young commoner called Arti who went to an isolated little spot in the Himalayas for a week. Not for rest and recreation, but to ideate. She'd had a mind block for months and her boss had warned her that if she didn't come up with an award-winning concept for Bye Bye Blood Suckers mosquito repellent, she could kiss her advertising career bye-bye.

Every morning after breakfast, Arti would sit at the edge of a pond with her iPad on her lap, a joint in one hand and a stress ball in the other. One day, she squeezed the stress ball so hard it bounced out of her hand and fell into the pond with a loud splash. Arti had a panic attack. There was no way she could replace her precious stress ball in this one-taxi town. Heck, they didn't even stock Sour Cream & Onion chips!

As tears started trickling down her cheeks, a croaky voice intruded on her thoughts.

'There, there,' it said sympathetically, 'if you miss your ball so much I can retrieve it for you.'

Arti looked down and her jaw dropped when she saw that it was a frog talking to her. She mentally scolded herself for chain-smoking local weed. She'd hoped that it would open her mind and show her fabulous visions that she could translate into out-of-the-box concepts for Bye Bye Blood Suckers mosquito repellent, and all it showed her was a stupid talking frog.

She ignored the frog and concentrated on her tears. The frog jumped on her lap, demanding attention. 'Hello, do you want that ball back or not?' it asked cheerfully.

'Get off my lap, you creepy thing,' Arti jumped up with a shriek.

'I'm not a creep,' the frog said morosely and its thick lips turned downwards into a pout. A teardrop shone in one eye.

Arti could feel her blood pressure sky-rocketing. Damn, she'd give anything to get her stress ball back. Even converse with a frog.

'Okay, you're not a creep, sorry. And if you can really get my ball back, I'll give you my Swatch watch, okay? It's waterproof,' Arti added in the wheedling tones of a salesperson.

'Nope, I don't need things. I'm rich,' the frog

immodestly said. 'All I want is to spend quality time with you.'

'Yeah yeah, whatever,' Arti waved it off impatiently.

The frog jumped into the pond and a second later it rose with Arti's stress ball in its mouth.

Arti thanked it politely and went back to her dingy hotel room. She spent the rest of the day scribbling some rubbishy ideas for Bye Bye Blood Suckers mosquito repellent. She smoked a few more joints and was relieved that no talking frogs intruded on her thoughts.

However, that night, when the room-service trolley was wheeled into her room, she was astonished to find the frog under a cloche.

Dammit, I overdid the weed again, she scolded herself.

'Ew, you look a mess – don't you dress for dinner?' the frog reprimanded her.

'Any more of your impudence and I'll be having tandoori frogs' legs instead of tandoori chicken for dinner, geddit?' Arti said menacingly.

The frog laughed. 'You're funny, I like that,' it said.

Arti ignored it and served herself. She'd barely had a bite when the frog jumped on her plate and started eating the chicken. Arti put the plate down with a shudder. No one in their right mind would eat food touched by a creepy animal, would they?

No matter, she consoled herself, *at least I'll lose weight this way*.

She got back to work and was astonished yet again when the frog plonked itself on her bed.

'I'm spending the night with you,' it said apologetically.

'Oh no, you're not!' Arti said firmly. 'Get out now or I'll get the hotel management to evict you!'

'But you promised me quality time,' the frog whined.

Arti gave in. Not because she was remotely interested in honouring her promises but because a germ of an idea had popped into her head.

'I'm not into bestiality so don't try anything funny,' she wagged a finger at the frog.

'Don't worry, you're not that hot,' the frog said sniffily and covered itself with the blanket.

The frog stayed with Arti for three days and nights. It even ate off her plate at breakfast, lunch and dinner but Arti didn't care. Mainly because she didn't notice. She was way too busy to eat, sleep, bathe or even watch TV. The germ of an idea was finally taking shape.

On the fourth morning, Arti cracked the concept! It was about talking mosquitoes and it was bloody brilliant. She was so excited, she picked up the frog from her pillow and kissed it – after all, she had to give credit where it was due.

And then she gasped because the frog suddenly turned into a sexy young man. He had thick, fleshy, froggy lips like Mick Jagger and Steve Tyler, and gosh, what a bod! *And what amazing weed!* Arti thought to herself. *I'm definitely taking some of that local shit back to the city!*

'Thanks babe,' the stunning male apparition said. Then he put her on his lap and started telling her some childish rubbish about being a prince who had been enchanted by a witch and had to share meals and spend three nights with a woman to become a prince again.

Who cares about a talking frog when there are SINGING frogs in the world?

Arti cut him short. 'Like, who cares?'

She leapt off his lap and started throwing things into her suitcase.

'So you'll marry me, of course, and then we'll go and live in my palace and produce little princes and princesses,' he said conversationally.

Arti froze. 'Marriage? Are you out of your tiny mind? I barely know you! Besides, I've got a fab career ahead of me and I bet my sweet ass that my talking mosquito ad campaign will win a Gold Lion at Cannes!'

She swept out of the hotel room with her suitcase, leaving a prince formerly known as frog behind. He looked hurt for a few minutes and then he shrugged it off. Big deal – she really wasn't that hot.

Moral: Mick Jagger and Steven Tyler have the only froggy lips that women want to kiss.

5

Fair & Lovely

Once upon a time, in a sleepy little kingdom in the Deccan Plateau, lived a tall, dark and average-looking king, his dusky queen and 365 concubines (one for each day of the year). This arrangement worked rather well because the Deccan queen complained of headaches every night and claimed that her European doctor had advised complete single-bed rest. So the king and queen happily went their own ways, till disaster struck one day: the queen was pregnant.

Now, let's establish some vitally important facts. The queen wasn't tall. Nor was she fair. Or even homely. And the less said about her tea-making and sitar-playing skills, the better. But she was 'convent-educated'. And it was this education that helped her convince the king that it was Immaculate Conception. Since the king himself had gone to a boarding school run by Jesuits instead of a posh boarding school for Indian princes, he bought the argument and enthusiastically invited three wise men from the West and the international media to witness the Second Coming.

The day dawned bright and clear. The king and queen huffed and puffed out their natural birth lessons when, suddenly, a shrill cry rent the air. It was the king who, thanks to his vantage point, first saw the baby's head emerging from the womb. It was covered with tight blonde curls. And its eyes were emerald green.

Admittedly, the king had failed his chartered accountancy exams seven years in a row. But he could put two and two together: the European doctor had abruptly left the country nine months ago + he had tight blonde curls + emerald green eyes = adultery.

The queen was beheaded. And the baby was called Fair & Lovely. The king couldn't bear to look at the queen's love child and packed her off to boarding school before she could say 'Papa'. The courtiers tut-tutted and said that if the baby had been a boy, perhaps ... but well, in his place they'd probably do the same thing.

The king married a fair-skinned Anglo-Indian with English, Portuguese and Dutch blood flowing through her veins. Of course, she also had her fair share of Tamilian blood, but she kept that a dark secret.

She bore him a son and made him very happy. She was reasonably happy too, till Fair & Lovely returned from boarding school at sweet sixteen. The cold mountain air had whipped up a gentle blush in her cheeks. Her blonde curls glittered in the sun. And her emerald eyes made the queen turn green with envy. What really got to her, however, was the fact that it was whispered that her skin was at least three shades darker than Fair & Lovely's.

'Mirror, mirror on the wall,' she screeched, 'who's the fairest of them all?' The mirror gulped and stuttered a reply, 'I cannot tell a lie, it's Fair & Lovely.' The queen turned purple with rage. She called Chota Elaichi, a hitman in Dubai, and agreed to pay him a king's ransom (well, actually, the princess's dowry) to do away with Fair & Lovely.

One dark evening, Chota Elaichi's hoods arrived at the palace gardens and kidnapped Fair & Lovely. Unfortunately for the queen, there was a shootout with a rival mafia gang in the concrete jungle outside the palace and Fair & Lovely managed to escape. She sought refuge in the house of seven Sherpas who willingly took her in because their last maid hadn't yet returned from a day's leave six months ago. So she cleaned and cooked fancy meals for them and in return got free boarding and lodging.

Meanwhile, the queen had got a new consignment of bleach, sunscreen with SPF 50+ and a range of yet-to-be-launched-in-India skin-lightening creams from her holidays abroad. After taking the prescribed seven-day fairness course, she decided to consult her mirror for the latest beauty update. Sadly, the answer was still Fair & Lovely. She turned purple with rage yet again, and flew to Dubai to confront Chota Elaichi. After getting her money back (with interest), she hatched a plot to get rid of Fair & Lovely herself.

She filled a vacuum cleaner with pest-control spray, disguised herself as a door-to-door salesman and knocked at Fair & Lovely's door. 'Try this, Meddem,' she said, 'it sure takes the aches and pains out of a broom.' Saying this, she switched the vacuum cleaner on and accidentally knocked off her false spectacles, nose and moustache. Fair & Lovely exclaimed, 'Why, Stepmama–' but she was cut short by the noxious pest-control spray. The queen watched with glee as Fair & Lovely writhed on the floor, coughing and choking. And when, after a final twitch she lay prone, the queen cackled and let herself out.

To say that the Sherpas were dismayed when

they saw her lying on the floor would be the understatement of the century. She was a model maid. No salary. No leave. No demands. She even cleaned the ceiling fans without being asked. The best part was, she didn't pinch their razors to shave her legs.

Sadly, they placed her body in a glass casket and put it in the garden as a lawn decoration piece. They stood back to admire it and were fairly pleased with the effect. Indeed, it looked far better than the usual hedges shaped like giraffes and lions. They wrote to *Homes & Gardens* and a photographer, Raj Kumar, was sent forthwith to cover their new garden ornament for the magazine's next issue.

The photographer instantly fell in love with Fair & Lovely's high cheekbones. He opened the casket to take a closer peek, and a whiff of his strong, cinnamon-scented aftershave jolted Fair & Lovely awake. She opened her emerald eyes, thought she was in heaven and he was God. They got married and she worshipped him till she discovered that he spent quality time on porn sites. After spotting his clay feet she treated him like an equal, which worked much better for both of them.

As for the king and queen, they lost all their money at the races and put the palace up for sale. Fair & Lovely and Raj Kumar bought it with a

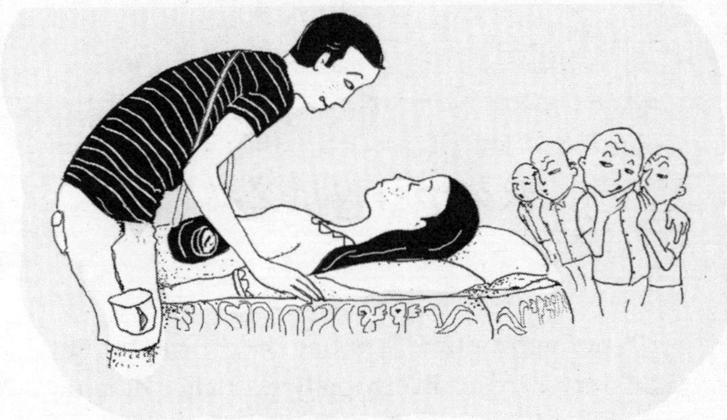

OMG! He's into necrophilia.

housing loan and turned it into a three-star hotel with hot and cold running water. They hired the seven Sherpas as hotel staff and they all lived happily ever after.

Moral: Don't fret over the colour of skin – remember it's the dark horses who always win!

6

Rapper N. Zel

Once upon a time, a young couple was trying very hard to live happily ever after despite their bitter fights over the TV remote control, when the wife fell ill. Her husband valiantly attempted to fix an appointment with several doctors but the waiting list was so long, the earliest one he got was for 7.45 pm five weeks later. In despair, he searched the Internet for her symptoms and discovered that a plant called rapunzel would cure his wife. He searched some more and found out that a crazy old lady in the neighbourhood grew the herb. It was rumoured that she had gone stark raving crackers after her head crashed against a glass ceiling in her office.

The young man rang her doorbell within minutes, ignoring the cardboard sign on the door that said, 'Men & other dogs not allowed'. The crazy old lady opened the door and glared at him: 'You can't read or what?'

The young man begged and pleaded and she finally relented, on one condition. 'You will give me your firstborn in exchange for a sprig of rapunzel, okay? But only if it's a girl. I hate boys – they grow up to be men,' she spat out.

The young man turned pale.

'If you really want a baby, why don't you adopt one?' he pleaded.

The crazy old lady put her hands on her hips and regarded him as though he was the one who was crazy.

'Oh, so you think adoption agencies in this country are willing to hand over babies to a single woman who's approaching menopause, is it?' she sneered.

The young man blushed. 'Sorry, that was a silly question,' he meekly conceded.

'See? See?' the crazy old lady shrieked, tearing tufts of hair out of her scalp. 'That's why I get so angry. Men are so stupid and yet they get to head companies and countries! Why? Why? Why?'

The young man trembled but stood his ground till the crazy old lady's fit of rage had subsided. After that, they went to a lawyer and an agreement was signed.

A year later, the young couple had a baby girl. The young man sent his wife to deliver the baby in a basket with a pretty pink ribbon – he was too terrified to face the crazy old lady himself.

The young woman begged the crazy old lady to allow her to meet the baby occasionally.

'Can't she spend every other weekend with us?' she wept.

The crazy old lady shook her head firmly and slammed the door.

Then she called a real-estate agent and asked him to find her a penthouse apartment in a skyscraper.

The baby was called Rapunzel, naturally. The crazy old lady loved her very much and was determined to shield her from evil, which is why Rapunzel was not allowed to meet men. She was locked up in the penthouse and had a TV, iPad, iPod and an Internet connection – what more could a girl ask for?

Rapunzel was a happy baby, and loved the lullabies the crazy old lady used to sing to her as she tucked her into bed.

Ain't no man good enough for my baby,
No, no, no.
If baby meets one, she'll turn his heart into pâté,
Yo, yo, yo!

However, after she became a teenager, Rapunzel's hormones started getting frisky. She had a massive, massive crush on the rappers she saw on TV. She wept when Jay-Z married Beyoncé. Besides, she'd written some cool rap songs herself and wanted to be a part of the scene. The crazy old lady refused.

'Absolutely not! You can't work in a male-dominated industry,' she said curtly.

Finally, Rapunzel had to resort to being slimy. She filmed herself performing her own rap songs and uploaded them on YouTube. She was an overnight hit and a young African-American producer called Shay-D got in touch with her. He wanted to sign her on and was willing to fly to India immediately. Rapunzel's heart sang and wept simultaneously. She wanted it so bad, but she couldn't escape. The penthouse door had a huge padlock on it. Then finally, she hit upon an idea: she called Shay-D and told him that if he wanted to meet her, she'd let down her hair and he could climb up 120 floors with the contract.

'You haven't cut your hair in nineteen years and it's as long as 120 floors?' Shay-D yelped with astonishment. 'Babe, I don't even want to think about your split ends! Besides, I'm not climbing up on a rope of hair to meet anyone. Not even Rihanna. How about you show me where your place is on Google Maps and I pick you up in a chopper?'

That's how Rapunzel escaped. She re-named herself Rapper N. Zel and became almost famous.

When you said you were coming with a chopper I thought you were going to give me a HAIRCUT!

A few years later, she discovered that Shay-D was pinching her profits and when she denounced him in public, every man in the industry turned against her. That's when the penny dropped. She went back to the penthouse in India and begged the crazy old lady for forgiveness. They set up a feminist website called weworkinournighties.com, and lived happily ever after.

Moral: Don't blame hormones – it's really glass ceilings that give women crazy feelings.

7

Thumbs Up

Once upon a time, long before artificial insemination and test-tube babies were heard of, there lived a frigid spinster who dearly wanted a baby. She frequently visited witch doctors and tried vile concoctions of dried batwings and suchlike but still couldn't conceive. The only certified doctor in the village prescribed sleeping with a male and recommended that she hang around pubs in fishnet stockings every evening for a month. She sharply said that she preferred swallowing fresh mongoose droppings to that option and slapped him with a sexual harassment suit.

One day, she chanced upon a fertility fairy and fell at her feet for help. The fairy gave her a cannabis seed with directions to water it twice daily. The frigid spinster nurtured it and sang rock ballads to it every day. Soon, a tiny bud appeared and its petals unfurled to reveal a beautiful little blonde flower child no bigger than a thumb. Which is possibly why she was named Thumbs Up. After all, frigid people have no imagination. They (hold your breath) even believe that the doctor and nurse uniforms in their hot-blooded friends' closets are solely reserved for fancy-dress parties.

The frigid spinster loved Thumbs Up with as much passion as she could muster. She gave her vitamins and made cute little clothes for her since she was too tiny (and too flat-chested, besides) to fit into Barbie's things. One night, while Thumbs Up was tucked into her little walnut-shell cradle fantasizing about some rock star or the other (hot vampire dudes hadn't made an appearance yet – I told you this story is ancient), a frog popped over the windowsill and fell madly in lust with her (proving the theory that even frogs prefer blondes).

He whisked her away and imprisoned her in a lilypad in the middle of the pond, informing her that their wedding was set for the next day. Thumbs Up totally freaked out and said, 'Cool it, Daddy O, I'm like, totally anti-institution.' (Hey, I *told* you this happened a long, long time ago – that's why even the language is seventies hippie-speak!) However, the frog was unmoved. He merely put her hysteria down to pre-wedding nerves and went ahead with the preparations.

If Thumbs Up had paid more attention during her transcendental meditation classes she may have been able to rise above her problems and the pond as well. But she hadn't. Helpless, she did what any other person in her position would do: she sang the blues. Now, we've often been told that there are lots of good fish in the sea. There are an equal number in ponds, too, and when they heard her mournful songs they decided to help spirit her away. They bit the stem off the lilypad and she floated into the sunset, promising to organize a Save the Goldfish march.

Once on dry land, she lived like a true flower child, eating magic mushrooms and making clothes for herself out of hemp. Her Earth Mother instincts won her many friends, including birds and bees (from whom she learnt everything her frigid mum didn't know about sex) and a gay mouse. She eventually moved in with the mouse because, as every woman knows, next to diamonds, gays are a girl's best friend. Life would have been groovy if it wasn't for the fact that the mouse's friend, Mr Mole, fancied her as a bride. (Yet again, we discover another disturbing fact about blondes: even blind creatures prefer them. Do they give out a scent or what?)

Feni, Vidi, Vici.

Thumbs Up asked one of her feathered friends to help her escape. He gave her a lift to Goa on a no-frills-no-mini-bottles-of-alcohol flight. They landed in a commune of flower children where Thumbs Up instinctively felt she had found her roots. The leader of the commune thought she was a heavy-duty chick and asked her to be his live-in dolly bird. She happily accepted because it was a real cool joint. They taught her to fly on marijuana instead of wings. Why, they even had a resident maharishi who was on first-name terms with rock stars.

So she changed her name to Mantra (her boyfriend thought Thumbs Up was too damn cute) and lived happily ever after, organizing protest marches all over the world.

Moral: If you pour peroxide on your head, you'll never go alone to bed.

8

The Ugh Duckling

Once upon a time, long before you, me or even the heroine of this story was born, there lived a vivacious duck called Duckie who fell madly in love with Rake, a handsome drake. Everybody warned her that he was only after *one* thing but she ignored them and foolishly went headlong into the relationship. So Duckie and Rake quacked their hearts out to each other and, finally, she let him have his wicked way. After about a year into their relationship, her biological clock started ticking so loudly, other ducks panicked and began to give her a very wide berth. They assumed she was a suicide bomber for some nasty terrorist group. Duckie knew she had to do something really quickly or else international intelligence agencies would be on her trail.

She tentatively broached the subject of marriage and spoke longingly about the patter of tiny webbed feet but Rake curtly said the world was overpopulated already and went back to his newspaper. She quietly went off the pill and soon started waddling about in an ungainly fashion. She knew she had to confess to Rake before the pretty embroidered pregnancy smocks came out. One night, after a torrid roll in the hay, she mustered up courage and told him she had a few buns in the oven. Rake said no thanks, he was on a zero-carb diet. Poor Duckie had to muster up some more courage to spell it out clearly. There was a pregnant silence. Then Rake quietly picked up his toothbrush and walked out of the house. Last heard of, he was living with a glamorous duck called Mona Darling.

So there was Duckie, pregnant and deserted. She laid her eggs in a shady nook near a pond and spent days keeping them warm and cozy while she flipped through child-care magazines and articles by feminists like Germaine Greer. Occasionally, ducks who were liberated enough to speak to an unmarried mother-to-be dropped by for a chat. One by one the eggs hatched and Duckie forgot her heartache and was happy and excited.

There was only one cloud on Duckie's horizon: the heroine of our story still wasn't born. She was in the last egg that stubbornly refused to hatch. Duckie started getting impatient. She hated being fat and frumpy. Indeed, once while glancing at her reflection in the pond, she was horrified to realize that she'd started looking like her mother: homely instead of comely. She wanted to get back to her svelte figure as soon as possible, but instead of swimming a hundred laps a day, she had to park herself on the egg like a couch potato and watch tedious re-runs of sitcoms on TV.

Finally, one bright sunny day, our heroine emerged from the egg. To say that she wasn't cover-girl material would be the understatement of the millennium. Next to her, even Frankenstein's monster looked stunningly gorgeous. She was a dingy grey instead of a cheerful sunshine yellow. To make matters worse, she had a blotchy red birthmark on one wing.

While Duckie was speechless, the other ducks started talking. Some said she was a bustard. Others said she was a bastard. All agreed that it was the same thing. And though Duckie did her best to protect her baby by loudly exclaiming, 'Don't you think she has her father's beak,' nobody was fooled.

Her siblings named her Ugh and teased her mercilessly about her looks. Even Duckie made it perfectly clear that she favoured her other ducklings. Ugh was very unhappy. On a cold day in December, Ugh decided that she couldn't take it any more. She picked up her meagre possessions and swam away from home.

She spent a few months doing solitary on a lake, swimming up and down to keep warm, when one morning she noticed some of the most beautiful birds she had ever seen in her life: they had long slender necks and were as white as snow. She thought she was dreaming and bent down into the water to splash her face when she was struck by her own reflection. She looked just like the beautiful birds around her. She assumed she had died of the cold without knowing it and this was her next avatar. Indeed, she had paid a heavy karmic price by having a miserable past life as an exceptionally ugly duckling. Suddenly, one of the graceful creatures glided up to her and politely asked to get a closer look at the birthmark on her right wing. Then she hugged her, saying, 'Yo, sistah!'

Ugh was perplexed, but the stranger showed her an identical birthmark on her right wing and said they were twins separated at birth, just like siblings in silly old-fashioned Bollywood movies. She took her to meet her real mother, a beautiful swan, who clasped her long-lost daughter to her bosom and said she had dropped her in Duckie's nest when she was just a little egg because she had been taught in school that you shouldn't put all your eggs in one basket. She wept and begged her to forgive a foolish old bird. Ugh tried to live happily ever after with her new-found family but didn't succeed – there was too much resentment bottled up inside her. She swam away and began her life yet again.

Soon after, Ugh was discovered by the PR agent for a ballet company. She became the mascot for international ballet troupes performing *Swan Lake* and frequently toured London, Paris, Rome, Tokyo and New York with the jet set. Her elegant new looks went to her head, and she dated furiously and dumped male swans equally furiously, earning the sobriquet of 'La Belle Dame Sans Merci'. After

Funny that success managed to get to your head, considering how far up the neck it had to travel!

ten years of smoking, drinking and partying like there was no tomorrow, age finally caught up with her. Ugh became puffy, florid and horizontally challenged: a lot like Elvis after he had buried his pelvis under junk food.

Once again, everyone made fun of her appearance. It was a déjà vu of her terribly unhappy childhood. Ugh was sacked and a younger swan replaced her as the ballet company's mascot. Oddly enough, Ugh didn't have a nervous breakdown. She calmly accepted her fate and got a new job as caregiver in a lunatic asylum called The Cuckoo's Nest. It was here that she finally lived happily ever after because everybody had way too many problems of their own to bother about foolish things like looks.

Moral: If you're born ugly, you cry far less when cruel age makes you look like a mess.

Acknowledgements

A big fat thank you to all the fabulous publications in which a few of the pieces in this collection made their debut. I have to confess, though, that I've made a few changes here and there. OCD, damn.

- 'Diet Wars' and 'Cindy' first appeared in *Verve*.
- 'Heavy Weather' made its first appearance in *Femina*.
- A part of 'Hell's Angel' was first serialized in *Deccan Chronicle*.
- 'Fair & Lovely' and 'The Ugh Duckling' first appeared on unboxedwriters.com.

Thanks and warm bear hugs to Viraj Rohan Circar for the jacket design and the fab illustrations and cartoons.

Here's to Saugata Mukherjee and Rachna Kalra at Pan Macmillan India who enthusiastically welcomed me on board. I'm still tapping my feet impatiently for that drink, though! And thanks to my meticulous, Pamuk-crazy editor, Pallavi Narayan.

Thanks to Dr Sunil Keswani for giving up an hour of his precious time for a discussion on sex change. Not for me – hey, I *love* being a girl – but for one of the characters in a story here.

And finally, cheers to my family and a friend for all their scathing criticism – and their tremendously helpful suggestions as well:

- Kushalrani Gulab aka Bunny and Salil Sadanandan: my worst critics. I still get feverish nightmares.
- Roma Circar, Mallika Circar and Ranjona Banerji: relatively kinder, sweeter critics – compared to the two horrors above!